Photo John Sculpher

Graham Sclater is based in Devon where he is a successful businessman and active in the local community. Prior to returning to Devon in the early seventies he was a professional musician playing all over the world and working as a session musician with numerous artists. His first novel *Ticket to Ride* first published in 2006 by Flame Books was recently republished by Tabitha Books. This was preceded by the novels *We're Gonna Be Famous* and *Hatred is the Key*. *Too Big To Cry* is Graham's fourth novel and he is currently working on his next novel *Love Shack* as well as a number of television and film scripts.

Other titles by the author

Ticket to Ride
We're gonna be famous
Hatred is the key

TOO BIG TO CRY

£

Graham Sclater

TABITHA BOOKS

Published in 2013 by Tabitha Books

Copyright © 2013 Graham Sclater

ISBN 978-0-9563977-5-1

Typeset in 12pt Sabon by
Kestrel Data, Exeter

Cover by Denise Bailey
Edited by Denise Bailey

Tabitha Books is a division of Tabitha Music Limited
Exeter EX2 9DJ England

TabithaBooks@tabithamusic.com

www.tabithabooks.webs.com

Tabitha Books © 2013

Acknowledgements

Denise who spent many weeks editing my words, Fedia Lavrov – my Russian buddy, Chris Bailey for her encouragement and belief, the Chamber of Commerce, Juan Artes for his support, Andrea Lownes, Antje Voit, Jimmy Jay, Phil Ray, JP and all the other radio presenters who have supported me with interviews and promotion.

CHAPTER ONE

Who will buy?

The vast tarmac car park that had been completely deserted an hour earlier was almost full and a line of queuing cars choked the nearby roads causing near chaos for other road users. In the heavy rain and strong winds the impatient drivers eventually began to pull in and fought to fill the spaces nearest to the main building. The occupants rushed out of their cars, joined the ever-growing crowd and pushed their way towards the open double doors.

As the rusty and faded pale green 1984-registered Vauxhall Astra turned into the car park, the driver braked hard and blocked the entrance. He pushed himself back into the seat and shook his head violently as he tried to take in the chaotic scenes around him. At the same time, he tried desperately to keep the engine ticking over, dropped the clutch and teased the accelerator pedal. A deafening roar reverberated throughout the car as, unable to hold back his anger any longer, he screamed out. 'Bloody leeches, they didn't waste any sodding time!'

His lapse in concentration caused the car to shudder to a standstill and it took several attempts before the engine turned over and he was finally able to make his way into the car park. He edged his way between the parked vehicles until he found the only remaining free bay at the far side of the car park alongside the row of identical vans. As he manoeuvred into the space, he scratched a shiny black BMW parked to his left. Once more his car stalled and he sat looking out through the dirty and cracked windscreen oblivious to the damage he had inflicted on the adjacent vehicle. Finding it extremely difficult to breathe he fumbled in the pockets of his jacket until he found his Ventolin inhaler. He pushed it between his quivering lips and squeezed it several times and waited until the drug took effect. He moved awkwardly across to the passenger seat and kicked the door open. Realising that he did not have enough room to squeeze out of the car, he reluctantly climbed back over the gear stick and hand brake into the driver's seat. He searched the glove compartment until he found the broken window winder, held it in place with his left hand while he wound down the window and then reached for the outside door handle. The rusty, misshapen door creaked loudly as he tried in vain to push it open. As his frustration grew he slid down into the seat, pushed his shoulder against the door until it swung forcefully into the van parked alongside it, the impact denting the bodywork.

Relieved but struggling to breathe he thrust his inhaler once more between his lips and pressed it a number of times and leaned against his car while he waited for the drug to take effect. The driver was a short man in his early forties, unshaven, with unbrushed collar length greasy dark brown hair greying at the temples and deep furrowed lines in his forehead. The ill-fitting creased check trousers, a ripped suede jacket, the torn lining hung down at the back and the mud splattered brown shoes appeared a ridiculous combination.

He stood and looked forlornly through his tired bloodshot eyes as the remnants of the crowd made their way excitedly towards the building. He finally pushed himself away from his car and as he walked between the dirty commercial vehicles he subconsciously ran his finger down the side of the nearest van to reveal unblemished paintwork. He pulled a filthy handkerchief from his jacket pocket and worked energetically rubbing at the dirt to reveal the shiny navy blue paintwork. Overcome with emotion he choked back the tears kicked at the tyres and walked slowly towards the front entrance. With his back bent and his narrow shoulders drooping forward he picked his way between the last row of cars stopping only for a brief moment to look up at the hand painted sign nailed to the side of the building – *Auction today*. Above it was a very impressive bright rectangular sign – **BCPS – Brian Chapman Property Services.**

Bending his head even lower he stooped unnecessarily and walked through the entrance. The large crowd, already assembled inside the building, were packed tightly together in what was previously the main office. Desks, chairs, filing cabinets, computers and all manner of office equipment was marked with a 'Lot number' and spread all around the office. The bespectacled middle aged auctioneer stood on a make-shift platform, a foot or so above the crowd and checked to see that anyone interested in the auction was inside. After clearing his throat, he began. 'Lot 1 – a four drawer filing cabinet. Let's start the bidding at twenty pounds'.

In the front of the crowd a young man shyly waved his catalogue while the auctioneer looked around the room for other interest. Although an overweight man joined in the bidding, at sixty-five pounds, he lost interest, allowing the younger man to complete the purchase and to smile nervously at the people nearest to him.

During the bidding for the first item, the dishevelled man pushed his way around the perimeter of the crowd and finding a place in a dark corner next to a bank of filing cabinets he removed a small notebook and pen from his inside pocket and began to write down the price of every item as it was sold.

Three hours later a hoarse but much-relieved auctioneer found his second wind and in a raised voice, he continued. 'Ladies and gentlemen, the penultimate item of the day Lot 427. What am I bid?'

The young assistant raised a fax machine above his head and the auctioneer continued. 'This is a very sophisticated piece of equipment,' he lied

The crowd had dwindled to only a few small groups of people who had little interest in the item. Many of the people chuckled to themselves at the auctioneer's outright exaggeration.

A woman in her mid-thirties nervously raised her hand. 'Thirty pounds!' she said.

The man in the shadows cursed under his breath as the auctioneer looked around the room and repeated the figure again. 'Thirty pounds, do I hear thirty five?'

A young man, raised his hand, but the young woman, after hesitating for a split second, continued to bid.

On the podium, the auctioneer sensed that the battle was almost over. 'Fifty five pounds, am I bid sixty?' He looked around the room but the interest had now diminished. 'Going once, going twice'. He raised his hand and smashed the gavel onto the desk. '. . . sold for ninety five pounds'.

The lady smiled and walked towards the auctioneer's clerk.

'Ladies and gentlemen we now come to the final lot of the day, lot 428,' said the relieved auctioneer. He looked across the room and the clerk held up a cardboard box and pulled out a letter opener and paper weight.

'This is a box of assorted items including this wonderful piece', said the auctioneer. He looked around the room but there was no interest whatsoever. A wry smile crossed his face. 'Ladies and gentleman surely there's someone who would like to own this?' He pushed his glasses up his nose and waited. 'Can I tempt anyone?

There was no interest.

He took a deep breath. 'Shall we say . . . a £1.00?'

The smartly dressed woman in the front row raised her hand nervously.

'Thank you . . .' said the relieved auctioneer. 'Do I hear two pounds?'

An elderly man raised his hand.

The auctioneer smiled.

'Do I hear three?'

The woman thrust her hand in the air and glared across at the elderly man.

The auctioneer tried to talk it up but there were no other bids and he brought the gavel down for the last time.

The woman tossed her head sideways as she sneered at the elderly man.

The much relieved auctioneer closed his book and took a deep breath before he spoke. 'Thank you ladies and gentlemen for attending today. If you could please make your way to the desk and settle your account and remove all items within the next hour.'

The woman smiled to herself as she made her way to pay for the box of miscellaneous items.

While the dishevelled man remained in the corner and concentrated on totalling the figures, the remaining members of the public made their way to the auctioneer's clerk to pay for the items they had bought. Shaking his head, the dishevelled man mumbled to himself. 'Three thousand, five hundred and twenty four pounds and fifty sodding pence, that's not going to go very bloody far'.

He thrust the notebook and pen into his pocket and walked slowly out of the room and through the remaining empty and deserted offices.

Looking into the last office he noticed a photograph on the floor behind the glazed door and bent down to pick it up. As he stopped to look at it the auctioneer's assistant walked into the room and confronted him.

'Can I help you, mate? What are you doing in here?' he demanded.

Still holding the photograph the man tried to hide it behind his back. 'It's alright . . .' He coughed nervously. 'It belongs to me,' he said softly.

'I think you must be mistaken, sir?' questioned the auctioneer's assistant.

'No . . . it is mine. I'm just having one last look ar . . .' mumbled the man in response to his interrogator.

The auctioneer's assistant smiled falsely, humouring him. 'Oh yeah . . . you are . . . are you?'

The man replied in an almost inaudible voice. 'I'm . . .' He cleared his throat and continued. 'I'm . . .' He paused once more and then continued. 'I'm . . . I'm, Brian Chapman'.

The auctioneer's assistant was taken aback and continued to

stare and not totally sure that the stranger was telling the truth continued to interrogate him. 'So you're Brian Chapman, eh?'

The stranger nodded, gave a forced smile, handed him the photograph and pointed to the smartly dressed man in the centre. The auctioneer's assistant cast his eye over the scruffy man standing in front of him. He studied the photograph more closely for a few seconds and finally satisfied with the man's explanation handed it back. 'Nice offices . . . it's a pity we didn't get more for this stuff and your vans. Mind you,' he sighed, 'yours is the ninth this week . . . you can't give anything away these days.

Brian stared at him while he felt in his pocket for the notebook. 'I know,' he said. He gave a half smile, turned and walked out of the room and down the corridor that had been his life for the last fifteen years. He stopped walking and glanced briefly at the photograph that had been taken only a few months earlier at the annual company dinner. He mumbled to himself. 'Those were the days'. He took one last look around the office and as he felt the tears welling up he walked slowly towards the main doors.

The auctioneer's assistant called after him. 'Bye, Mr Chapman'.

Without any acknowledgment or response Brian, hunched and defeated, continued walking and left the building. Standing alone he pulled the filthy handkerchief from his pocket and wiped his eyes. He took a deep breath, straightened his back and walked slowly across the now deserted car park towards his car.

The grey sky darkened and the rain laden clouds driven on by the strong south westerly wind built up above him and it started to rain heavily. Still clutching the rolled up photograph he ran towards his car and he made a pathetic attempt to protect himself from the elements by pulling his narrow jacket collar up around his neck.

An ear-splitting shot reverberated across the car park. Brian slumped forward and fell heavily to the ground and the photograph propelled by the strong wind blew out of his hand and across the car park.

CHAPTER TWO

Holding back the tears

The car park was packed with immaculate navy blue company vans and more than two dozen engineers wearing clean matching uniforms talked animatedly to each other. The video director anxiously planned a series of shots with his cameramen and crew. A tower had been erected in one corner of the car park and accommodated the first camera and sound crew, while a second crew was positioned in the back of a pick-up truck ready to follow the vans.

'Could I have a bit of time to think here gents?' boomed the video director.

The engineers stopped talking and stood to attention.

'Thank you'. He smiled and nodded. 'OK . . . we'll go for a take . . .' He paused. 'Remember don't all rush to get out of the car park. Take it leisurely and we'll try . . .' He looked around at his crew and continued. '. . . to shoot this in one'.

The engineers, clearly nervous, looked at each other and held their breath.

'Quiet please!' boomed the director. He looked around to

his cameramen, and when they nodded their readiness, he turned. 'And . . . action!' he boomed.

Craig Jameson, a smartly dressed man, in his mid-thirties, walked out of the office and made his way to the small group of engineers. He handed out the job sheets to the engineers and as instructed made a few exaggerated gestures and, as the vans slowly drove out of the car park the pick-up with the second cameramen followed, he walked back towards the office.

Out of shot, a navy blue Audi saloon drove in and parked on the edge of the car park.

Brian Chapman, wearing a tailored double breasted grey suit with a blue striped shirt and dark blue patterned tie, acknowledged the director and crew as he walked towards his office.

The office was buzzing, the service centre printers spewed out orders, the phones rang as soon as they were replaced and there was intense activity throughout the building.

Brian entered his secretary's office.

'Morning Jackie, it's a bit hectic out there today,' he said with a smile.

Jackie, in her late forties with dark brown shoulder length hair, was smartly dressed in a burgundy suit and white blouse.

'Morning Brian . . . Yes, I know. I came in especially early today to get a parking space'. She looked at the notes on her desk. 'Oh . . . by the way, don't forget you're interviewing Mr Corke at nine,' she said.

'No problem. Let me have a quick coffee and when he arrives send him straight up'.

'Fine,' she replied brightly. 'I've left the post and important emails on your desk'.

*

Brian entered his conservatively decorated and tidy office. He liked it that way, plain walls with photographs of woodland scenes he had taken in the spring hung on every wall and huge plants filled every corner. The walls were painted pale blue and yellow divided by a white dado rail. Dark blue carpets and two pale blue leather settees, a matching armchair and a large glass coffee table was positioned near the door while at the other end of the office his desk took pride of place near the window. He had chosen to place it there so he could look out onto the car park and keep an eye on any of the engineers who were in the car park and, not out earning him money.

He sat at his desk and began to open the post. Brian religiously opened the post himself; it was his way of keeping track of things, an immediate indication of the condition of the business. He could see at a glance how many orders were coming through and how many invoices were being paid. His accountant, David Thornton, had told him many years before that any *businessman* should be able to calculate where his business was at any time, something he had never forgotten but recently had found more difficult to put into practise.

Jackie knocked and entered with Brian's coffee.

He took it from her and as she left he moved away from his desk and gazed out of the window. As he sipped at his coffee a proud look of achievement crossed his face. He took a couple of sips and sat back at his desk to continue to open the post.

The phone rang.

'Mr Corke for you, Brian,' said Jackie.

Brian waited for Jackie to knock his door and he stood up.

'Mr Corke,' said Jackie.

Brian glanced up at the clock, smiled and reached out and

shook his hand. 'Pleased to meet you, Mr Corke did you manage to find a parking space?'

Mr Corke, in his late fifties, dressed in dark trousers, a polo shirt and a sports jacket, appeared very nervous. 'Yes I did'. He forced a smile. 'Um . . . down the road . . . that's why I was a few minutes late,' he replied apologetically.

Brian checked the clock again.

Jackie smiled at him.

'That's not a problem,' said Brian acknowledging him with a nod. 'It's not your fault'.

'I know . . . but first impressions and all that . . .' replied Mr Corke as his voice tailed off.

Brian smiled.

'Why all the activity?' asked Mr Corke.

'We're making a promo video . . . you need it to get the name out there on the web. It's a competitive world and we want to be part of it,' he said. 'But it's not cheap . . .' Brian sipped at his coffee and stopped suddenly. 'I'm sorry,' he said apologetically. 'Would you like one?' he asked raising his empty mug and looking across at Jackie.

'Yes please,' replied Mr Corke. '. . . milk and two sugars'.

Jackie left the office and Brian sat back in his leather executive chair. 'Please take a seat,' he said.

Mr Corke sat down and while Brian scanned the application form he smiled to himself as he checked out the office.

'Excellent . . .' said Brian clearly impressed. 'I see you've worked for a number of service companies'.

'Yes . . . but . . .' Mr Corke started to tremble. 'I've been made redundant twice in the last few months,' he said, clearly upset. 'They all seem to make the same mistakes—'

'Um,' said Brian with an extended sigh.

18

There was a knock at the door and Jackie entered with a tray and placed two matching cups and saucers on Brian's desk, picked up the empty mug and smiled at Mr Corke as she left.

'Tell me, Mr Corke, what do you know about us?' asked Brian.

'Well . . .' He pushed himself into the chair. 'I know you set up the company in 1995'. He paused. 'I've been watching you grow over the last few years'. He sucked in air nervously. 'It's been very impressive'.

Brian smiled proudly.

'Thank you,' said Brian. He paused as he fiddled with the unopened letters and squared up the envelopes, tapping them gently on his desk. 'As you know we work exclusively for blue chip multi-national clients who want service and a professional job'. He pushed the neat pile of envelopes across his desk. 'We've got to get it right . . . if there's a sniff of a problem we *know* we won't get paid'.

Brian looked hard at Mr Corke and waited for a reaction.

Mr Corke nodded his reserved agreement.

'We don't use many sub-contractors; predominantly it's directly employed labour. That way we can plan our workload and be sure we won't let our clients down and . . .' He sighed heavily. 'We'll get paid . . . and you'll get your wages at the end of the week. Does that sound reasonable?'

Mr Corke smiled before he replied. 'I would like the opportunity to work for you, Mr Chapman and . . .' He thought hard before he continued. 'Maybe this will be third time lucky and I can break the jinx'.

'I hope it will be too,' replied Brian.

Brian placed the C.V. neatly on his desk and pushed himself away from his desk. 'Can you start on Monday?'

Mr Corke smiled broadly and nodded excitedly.

Brian picked up the telephone. 'Jackie, can you pop up please,' he said.

While they were waiting for Jackie, Brian continued to open the post, stopped and reread the letter in his hand. He thought to himself for a few seconds before he looked up. He paused again before he finally spoke. 'Tell me, Mr Corke . . .' Brian paused and looked directly at Mr Corke before he continued. 'How do you feel about . . .' he gazed at Mr Corke before he continued. 'Repossessions?' he said slowly.

Mr Corke fidgeted uncomfortably in his seat. 'Well . . . I'm not sure how you want me to answer that one?' he asked.

'I understand,' said Brian. 'It's not the sort of business we would normally consider'. His thumb stroked the embossed print on the letterhead. 'But it looks like we've got a new client, good one at that . . . and there could be a steady volume of business coming our way'.

'Well, work is work but I'd hate it to happen to me,' said Mr Corke looking decidedly uneasy.

Jackie walked into the office and sensed the change in atmosphere. 'Is everything all right?' she asked.

'Yeah, it's fine,' said Brian holding up the letter. 'It looks like we've won the contract with the Southbourne Building Society.

'Repossessions?' asked Jackie.

'That's the one,' replied Brian putting the letter back on his desk. He turned to Mr Corke and then to Jackie. 'Good news.' He smiled broadly. 'Mr Corke will be joining us on Monday'.

Jackie and Mr Corke smiled at each other.

'Could you take him to the 'ops' office, introduce him

to Craig and ask him to explain the procedures and make arrangements for his van'. Brian stood and shook Mr Corke's hand firmly. 'Good to have you with us, see you on Monday'. He turned. 'Oh . . . and don't worry too much about the repossession work, I don't think things are going to get that bad'.

'Thank you, Mr Chapman'. Mr Corke nodded appreciatively. 'Thanks very much.' He followed Jackie out of the office and pulled the door behind him.

The phone on Brian's desk rang. He flicked at the phone and spoke on it hands free. 'Hello'.

'It's Mr Simms from the bank for you, Brian,' said the female voice at the other end.

'Put him thorough,' he said. He waited a few seconds before he answered. 'Hello Harry . . . how are you?'

'Fine thanks Brian'.

'Did you get to play at the weekend?'

'No . . . it was Doreen's birthday so we went to Bath'.

'Did she like her present?'

'Yes.' He laughed to himself. 'Oh . . . sorry Brian, she asked me to thank you . . .' He smiled to himself. 'Nice thought'. He paused. 'So . . . how's business?'

Brian replied with a chuckle. 'Not bad . . . could be better . . . but I'd always say that wouldn't I?'

'How much are you banking today, Brian?' asked Harry.

'I've just been through the post and BACS payments . . . not a lot . . . about fifteen hundred . . . clients aren't rushing to pay us these days . . .' He lowered his voice. 'You know what it's like?'

Harry didn't reply.

'Are you still there Harry?'

'Yes Brian . . . I'm here, but that's not going to go very far is it?'

Brian suddenly felt uncomfortable. 'Well probably not,' he said. 'But we've been promised thirty thousand from Sanders and . . . we've just won a contract with the Southbourne Building Society'. He paused and smiled broadly. 'Repossessions,' he replied enthusiastically.

Harry cleared his throat. 'Sorry Brian, but we have a problem. If I put through the cheques for the VAT and PAYE you'll be well over . . .'

Brian could hear Harry punching his calculator and he reached for his inhaler and pressed it twice in quick succession.

Harry continued. 'It's thirty eight thousand for just those and I know you've got the wages in a couple of days and, with the leased vehicle payments . . . you'll be well over your agreed limit'.

Brian grabbed the handset. 'Bloody hell!' he said.

He tore at his hair.

'But you've got to put those through, Harry!'

'Brian, I'll tell you what I'll do'. He suddenly stopped and paused.

Brian tapped at his desk impatiently and muttered to himself as he waited for the banker to continue.

'I shouldn't . . . but I'll try and hold them back until tomorrow . . . Come in and see me on Thursday at . . .'

Brian could hear him tapping at the keys on his computer.

'Ten . . . and we'll go through things then'. He cleared his throat. 'I'm going to email you some forms. If you can complete them . . . every section, and bring them with you, it will give me a better feel for things'.

Brian sighed heavily. 'Alright, Harry, see you on Thursday

but please don't let me down'. Unable to hide his anger he paused and took a deep breath. 'You know what will happen if you return *those* cheques don't you?' he said as his voice faded.

'See you on Thursday, Brian,' said Harry as he replaced the receiver.

With the phone still in his hand Brian wrote the appointment in his desk diary and scribbled a note for Jackie. He pondered for a few seconds and pressed the phone.

'Yes, Brian?'

'Pam, can you print out the sales ledger and bring it up here as quick as you can'.

'I'll be about then minutes,' she said.

Brian sat back in his chair and tapped his pencil erratically on the desk before thumbing through the post once more and talking to himself. 'What the *hell* am I going to do?' he mumbled.

He pushed himself away from his desk looked out onto the car park and watched the first cameramen shooting close-ups of his engineers and vans. At the end of the shot they all broke into raucous laughter. He grimaced and muttered to himself as he slowly shook his head. 'None of you give a *fuck* as long as you get paid . . . do you?'

There was a knock on his door but he didn't hear it. He was angry and deep in thought.

There was another knock but he was still oblivious to it.

'Brian'.

Pam knocked again, opened the door and raised her voice. 'Brian!'

Brian turned.

'Oh . . . sorry Pam'. He looked up at her.'

'You've got the ledger?'

She nodded.

Pam, in her late thirties had her dark hair pulled back in a French plait and wore a dark clinging jumper, short dark skirt and very high heels. She wore little makeup but still looked very attractive.

'Good. Let's have a look,' he said as he reached out and took it from her.

Pam sat opposite him and eyed Brian intently as he flicked through the reams of paper and totalled up the amounts on an invisible calculator. At every turn of the page his expression changed as he became more and more concerned.

Pam pointed at a long line of outstanding invoices from one client. 'We should have taken *them* to Court,' she said.

'You know what would have happened if we had?' he said. 'Remember . . . we tried it with Harrison's and they stopped using us'. He paused and reflected. 'Well, not completely'. He shook his head and gave a wry smile. 'Just enough to keep us hanging in there eh?' He tapped the page heavily. 'Look at these!' he said holding up the print outs. 'Fifteen thousand . . . eighty . . . forty five . . .' He turned another page. 'Look at this . . . sixty three thousand!'

He threw the ledger across the office and the concertina of paper opened and spread across the carpet.

Pam fidgeted nervously in her chair before she spoke. 'Brian, you know we've both been chasing all of them every day—'

'I know . . . and every day we get promises . . . and more promises,' he said raising his voice.

He stood up, took a deep breath and straightened his jacket.

'OK . . . this is what we're going to do'. He picked up the ledger, straightened the pages before he ripped it in half, and spread one half across his desk. 'Right, Pam. The situation we've got with Harry is bloody serious. If we don't get some cash in tomorrow I think we can wave all this goodbye'. He extended his arms and pointed at the window. 'I'm not going to let that happen,' he said.

He forced a smiled. 'All right?'

Finding it hard to hold back the tears, Pam covered her face and left the office in silence.

CHAPTER THREE

Every little bit hurts

Pam sat at her desk, replaced the handset, made notes on the ledger and immediately dialled the next number on the list. As Jackie entered the office Pam slammed down the phone.

'Are you alright?' asked Jackie.

Pam glared back at her.

Jackie looked at her apprehensively and spoke softly. 'How *is* it going?' she asked.

'Shit . . . It's bloody ridiculous. I've spoken to more than fifteen clients and they're all coming up with the same excuses'. She mimicked their voices. 'Director's on holiday . . . Financial Director's off sick . . . Surveyor hasn't signed them off . . . Haven't received the invoices . . .' She slammed her hand on the desk. 'It's crap . . . I've already faxed, emailed and posted copies to them all at least half a dozen times!'

Jackie sat on the corner of Pam's desk.

'I know what it's like my sister's boyfriend has got the same problem with his business. It's ludicrous; the excuses people keep coming up with'. She looked into space. 'I just don't believe any of them'.

The phone rang on Pam's desk. 'Hello . . .' She nodded. 'OK Brian, I'll be right up'. She replaced her phone and made a grotesque face to Jackie.

'Is it really that bad? asked Jackie.

Pam didn't reply and left the office.

She knocked on Brian's door and entered. Brian was talking on the telephone. 'We've already sent you two sets of invoices . . . I'm not interested in your fucking computer!' He screamed with rage. 'When the hell are you going to pay them?' He tapped on his desk as he listened to the accounts clerk on the other end before he continued. 'I tell you what you're going to do!' he screamed. 'You'll call me back in an hour and tell me how much you'll be transferring—'

The clerk interrupted him and Brian slammed his free hand hard on his desk.

'I don't want a fucking cheque! I want the money transferred!' He spluttered with rage. 'And, I want to know *when*! Understand!' He clenched his fist. 'If not, I will personally come up there and sit in reception until you bastards pay me . . . Got that! And I'll have my guys rip out the phone system we've just fitted at your new store!'

He slammed down the phone.

'The bastard!' he screamed. 'Bloody bastard!' he wiped the anger from around his mouth. 'Leaving kids . . . to do a man's job, what the . . . ?' He looked up. 'Oh . . . sorry, Pam'. He pushed himself away from his desk and slid across to her in his chair.

'How did you get on?'

He stood up and slowly shook his head.

'Dare I even ask?'

Pam looked at him nervously. 'I'm sorry . . . we've had the

same responses . . . although . . .' She paused and forced a token smile. 'I have had promises on a few of the bigger ones'.

'Let's see if they do what they say,' he sighed.

'Dealing with these people is . . .' She paused and thought. 'They're faceless you know. They all pass the buck . . . blame someone else . . .' She grimaced. '. . . just want to get you off the phone'.

Brian looked across the office at the framed company photographs on the wall above the coffee table. He straightened one of them and slumped back into his chair. 'That's all well and good but its companies like us that are going to the wall'.

There was a knock at the open door and Jackie walked in carrying an armful of paper.

'Here we are, Brian. This came from the bank'.

'Thanks, Jackie, put it on my desk'.

Pam stood up.

'No, Pam, stay where you are, we need to go through this while you're here'.

Pam blushed nervously and sat down.

Brian reached for his now cold coffee, took a huge gulp, frowned and slammed it down. He flicked through page after page of the questions emailed from the bank. 'We're going to have our work cut out here. Pam, you fill in the sections you can, bring it back and we'll complete the rest'.

There was another knock at the door.

Jackie walked in followed closely by the video director, cameramen and crew.

'Hi, Brian, we're about wrapped up outside, could you do your interview now?' asked the director.

Jackie looked at Pam and then turned to Brian. 'Are you sure?' she mouthed.

Brian smiled. 'Yeah, course you can,' he said. 'I'll be fine'.

Brian looked across at Jackie and gave her a reassuring look and mouthed to her. 'Coffee?'

Jackie picked up the cup from the desk, nodded and left with Pam.

Jackie sat on the edge of Pam's desk. 'How on earth is he going to pick himself up with all the other nonsense going on?'

'I'm sure he will,' said Pam.

'I hope so . . . he's at the bank on Thursday, said Jackie'. She suddenly jumped off the desk. 'Oh, I nearly forgot Brian's coffee,' she said rushing off to the kitchen.

Brian's office was soon a mass of cables as the crew set up the lighting and positioned the microphones while the director agreed on the camera angles. Brian sat at his desk and tried desperately to gather his thoughts. He slid his laptop across to one side of his desk and rearranged his pens and moved them once more before putting them back in the original position.

While Brian continued to rearrange the papers on his desk the video director spoke to him and placed a vase of fresh flowers strategically at one corner. 'I reckon the car park scenes will work really well. You've certainly got a good bunch of guys, Brian,' he said enthusiastically.

Brian nodded and forced a smile.

'From what I've seen so far . . . an excellent company,' continued the director.

'Thanks,' said Brian. He sighed heavily. 'But I should be saving money, not spending it'.

'I'm sure you're right, but it's companies like yours who look ahead that are going to get through the recession first . . . not those that bury their heads in the sand,' said the cameraman.

Brian looked up at him and replied as he rearranged his tie. 'Maybe . . . but sometimes I do wonder'.

In the operations office Craig Jameson shook Colin Corke's hand. 'See you on Monday, Colin. I should come in about nine . . . that'll give us a chance to get the guys out . . . Bye'.

Colin Corke walked out into the car park whistling a celebratory tuneless high pitched noise.

Natasha, the young eighteen year old trainee, walked in with a cup of coffee and passed it to Craig.

'What's it like being a film star,' she asked coyly.

'I take it all in my stride,' he bragged.

Natasha hung on his very word and stood near the door. 'Do you think you could get me in it?' she asked.

'Course, why not,' he replied.

'You'll let me know which day won't you? Tell me what you want me to wear'.

Craig looked at her and winked. 'I wouldn't wear anything'.

Natasha blushed and left the office.

The engineer flicked a switch and Brian was suddenly engulfed in bright light. He closed his eyes briefly before reopening them and squinting at the director. As soon as Brian was accustomed to the light the director spoke to him off camera.

'Could you tell us the secret of your success?' he asked.

Brian thought and answered. 'We've always said that our client is King, and they need a company that can supply them with a professional and quality service. No nonsense and value for money. We've been in business since 1995 and our client base speaks for itself but . . .' Brian stopped himself and was ready to say – *if they paid their fucking bills, wouldn't it be great?*

'Cut!' shouted the director. 'Would you like to do that again, Brian?'

Brian looked at him and nodded. 'Please'.

The director looked down at his notes. 'Brian, continue from client base'. He turned to the crew. 'Take two!'

Brian reflected before speaking. 'Our blue chip client base speaks for itself. We've got it right and we've also been certified with ISO accreditation, which underlines our quality'.

'Cut!' shouted the director. 'Excellent Brian, that'll do. We'll shoot some on site stuff now. Is there anything else you want to add?'

Brian suddenly looked tired and drawn. 'No, I don't think so,' he said.

The crew rushed around his office, rewound the cables onto huge reels and dismantled the lights. When they'd finished the cameraman reached across the desk and shook Brian's hand. 'Nice to meet you, Mr Chapman'.

Brian sat at his desk and continued to check and double check the extensive list of debtors.

'Why can't the big bastards pay on time?' he seethed as he dialled the next number on his list.

Jackie knocked and entered.

'How did it go?'

Brian replaced the handset. 'Fine . . . it was difficult to concentrate . . . but I think I did all right'.

He walked across the office and sat next to her on the settee. He loosened his tie and undid his top shirt button before he took the partially completed forms from her, filled in the missing figures, and sat back. 'OK, I've just put in our creditors from Pam's ledger and I reckon we're going to need . . .' He checked his invisible calculator. 'I reckon two hundred thousand to get through this . . .' He sighed. 'Plus we need to pay for the bloody video . . .'

'How on earth are we going to get that sort of money when there's a recession out there?' asked a shocked Jackie.

Brian shook his head. 'I've got to try, what else can I do?'

Jackie smiled back at him nervously.

CHAPTER FOUR

Money can't buy me love

David Thornton's austere client meeting room at the rear of his offices looked exactly the same as it had back in the mid-nineties when Brian visited him for the first time to ask for his help to set up his own company. The wallpaper was faded and the woodwork scratched and flaking. The carpet was threadbare and the only furniture in the office was the badly scratched oak desk and two odd chairs given to him by his clients. Displayed in pride of place was an antique 1899 Wellington 2 thrust action typewriter on its original hardwood base; a collection of handwritten ledgers, quills and ink.

Brian had been working for a national maintenance company but felt the time was right to do something on his own. He met David at a charity boxing event at the university the week before Christmas 1994, and by the end of the evening Brian knew what he was going to do. The next morning Brian discussed it with Sylvia, his pregnant wife, and whilst she had concerns about him leaving the stability of a full time job she realised that Brian had set his heart on running his own company. David worked with Brian for months to develop his business plan; arrange a second mortgage of £25,000 and set up a meeting with Harry Sims at the Alford Bank. Harry agreed an overdraft of £25,000, which was guaranteed by the bank taking a second charge on the family home. The rest was a formality and in May 1995, within a few days of Jamie's birth, Brian Chapman Services Limited was incorporated. David arranged for Brian to take a lease on one of the new units he was developing and the following month the business started to trade.

David's motto was clear. *'Don't waste money on things that don't earn you anything.'*

Brian had followed that principle throughout his business until he took the decision to make the promotional video.

David stood up from behind the desk and reached out to shake Brian's hand.

'Hello, Brian, it sounded urgent?'

Brian nodded.

'I've got a real problem'. He blushed nervously. 'Harry is threatening to bounce the VAT and Revenue cheques'.

'How much?' asked his accountant.

'Close to forty grand'. Brian paused and took a deep breath. 'And I've got the wages this week and lease payments on the six new vans next week'.

'Um...' David looked up from his desk and made no attempt to hide his concern. 'You realise, if he does refer them you'll have a major problem?'

Brian closed his eyes and nodded slowly.

'He sent me this,' said Brian.

He passed the completed forms across the desk. 'I reckon we're two hundred grand light'.

'If it is any consolation . . .' David looked at Brian and shook his head. 'The blood sucking bastards are treating the majority of our clients the same'.

David rechecked the figures and took a deep breath. 'Yeah . . .' He nodded. 'You need at *least* two hundred'. He sat back in his chair and thumbed through his cardex. 'I know someone who's got an in with City Investors and Venture Capitalists but it's going to mean letting go some of the equity in the business and paying upfront fees'. He stared hard at Brian. 'How do you feel about that?'

'Have I got an option?'

David didn't answer, instead he tapped his desk. 'Leave it with me. His name's Nicholas Henley. If I can get hold of him, I'll ask him to call you later'.

A dejected Brian walked slowly out of the office.

David shouted after him. 'Don't worry . . . you're not the only one'.

'That's exactly what I am worried about,' muttered Brian as he walked down the corridor.

Brian sat at his desk and concentrated while he checked and rechecked the sales and purchase ledgers on his laptop.

Jackie walked through the open door and moved close to his desk. 'Can David help?' she asked.

'I don't know, I really don't know'. He shook his head and then looked up. 'But I am expecting a call later from a financial advisor'. He forced a smile. 'According to David he's got an in with some influential people in London so let's see what he can do'.

Brian looked across at Jackie, closed his laptop, laid down his pen and reorganised his desk. He looked long and hard at the vase of flowers placed on his desk by the video director.

Jackie pointed at the flowers and smiled. 'I like those on there, a nice touch'. She slid her fingers sensuously along the petals.

Brian ignored her and suddenly stood up.

Jackie stepped back and as she stiffened let the flowers slip through her fingers.

'That's it! I can't do any more today and I can't go home like this . . . who knows what I'd do'.

Jackie looked at him intently and stroked her lips evocatively before she smiled kindly.

Surprised at her response he screwed up his face. 'I've got to get this shit out of my system. Sod it . . . I'm going to the gym'.

Brian picked up his leather case and walked towards the door. He stopped and turned. 'Sorry, Jackie,' he said softly. He tilted his head to one side. 'Oh . . . there is one thing you can do for me'.

Jackie smiled at him expectantly.

'Can you find out who I need to speak to at the HMRC? I'll give them a ring first thing in the morning to pre-empt them calling us'.

She didn't hide her disappointment.

'Sure, Brian,' she said as she dropped her arms to her side. 'They'll be on your desk in the morning'.

Brian signalled and drove up the short drive towards the three bedroomed detached house in a quiet cul-de-sac of a handful of identical properties. He sat in the car and looked up at the only house he and Sylvia had ever lived in and sighed heavily.

The music faded and the radio announcer spoke. 'Here is the six 'o clock news. A further two thousand workers have been laid off by . . .'

Brian punched at the radio, locked the car and spent a few minutes walking around his garden. He liked gardening and after dead heading a few roses he carefully picked a handful of penstemons and walked through the gate and into the back garden.

Jenny, his six year old daughter, was sitting on the swing holding her doll. She was still wearing her school uniform, a pale blue blouse and navy blue skirt and white socks. Her curly blond hair fell across her tiny shoulders and her long fringe partially covered her dark blue eyes. As soon as she saw her father she pushed her fringe aside, shot off the swing and ran towards him.

'Hello, daddy . . . you *are* early tonight,' she said excitedly.

Brian smiled at her. 'It's good to come home early sometimes, eh poppet?'

'Jamie's out with his friends, daddy'. She pulled a face and continued. 'But guess what?' she teased.

'I don't know'. He pulled a face back to her. 'Why you don't tell me?'

'We . . . ll, mummy's cooking your favourite . . .' She waited for Brian's reaction but he feigned knowing the answer. Jenny continued. 'Chicken casserole . . . silly,' she said with an infectious giggle.

She continued to giggle as she launched herself into his arms. He put down his case and flowers and swung her around. 'Come on let's see if your mother really is cooking what you say,' he said stretching every word.

'She is . . . she is . . . you'll see!' screeched Jenny.

Brian put his finger over her lips. 'Well then, let's surprise her shall we?'

Sylvia was standing over the hob stirring the casserole and was startled when Brian and Jenny crept in. 'Brian, you frightened me,' she snapped. 'What are you doing home so early?'

'Did we really frighten you, mummy?' shrieked Jenny.

'Of course you did, I nearly jumped out of my skin,' she lied.

'We didn't frighten you too much, did we?' asked a concerned Jenny.

'No . . .' She faked a scowl. 'Course you didn't'.

Sylvia kissed Brian on the cheek and he handed her the flowers.

'They're lovely aren't they, Jenny? Would you like to put them in a vase for me?'

Jenny knelt down and searched through the cupboard for a suitable container to put them in.

Sylvia turned to Brian. 'How are you, darling? Everything all right?' she mouthed.

He looked at her. 'It's been a sh . . .' He stopped abruptly and forced a smile before he looked down at Jenny and continued. 'A terrible day,' he said.

'Daddy, were you going to say something naughty then, weren't you?' quizzed Jenny.

'Go and play in the garden, Jenny. I'll call you when it's ready,' said Sylvia sternly.

'What about the flowers?' she shrieked.

'It's all right, I'll do that,' said her mother.

Jenny raced out into the garden and jumped back onto the swing.

Sylvia looked concerned. 'I thought you were filming the

video today, you told me you were looking forward to it'.

'Yeah, we were and it's going really well but I had a call from Harry Simms—'

'And?' She asked apprehensively. 'He was all right wasn't he? He's always saying how—'

Brian interrupted her and nodded. 'I know that, but he says he's going to return a couple of cheques . . .'

Sylvia then interrupted him. 'That's terrible? I thought . . .' Her hands started to tremble.

Brian reached out and squeezed them tightly. 'I don't know. I've been to see David this afternoon and he says he knows someone who can help us'.

Sylvia nodded. 'So it's not that bad then?' She turned to stir the casserole. 'Get changed and we'll have dinner in the garden tonight'.

'Shall I open a bottle of wine?' asked Brian.

Sylvia smiled. 'Why not?' she said. 'Go on and get changed or this will be ruined,' she said as she furiously stirred the casserole.

Brian changed into a tee-shirt and chinos and returned to the kitchen. He opened a bottle of red wine and poured two glasses and handed one to Sylvia.

'Cheers'.

Sylvia smiled. 'Cheers,' she said. 'I bet you feel better all ready? Right?'

'Right,' he lied.

Jenny rushed into the kitchen. 'Look what I did at school today, daddy,' she screeched as she held up a drawing. 'Do you like it?' she asked excitedly.

'That's very good, Jenny'.

'It's our family and I've even got Sammy in it,' she said excitedly

Brian looked at the picture, turned it around and then upside down. 'It's nice. Sammy looks more like himself than anyone else'.

'I know . . .' she said softly, 'but dogs are easier to draw than people'.

Brian and Sylvia laughed loudly and he refilled his glass, drank it and smiled.

'Come on Jenny, why don't you and daddy set the table outside?' coaxed Sylvia.

She didn't need to say any more. Jenny carefully selected the cutlery from the drawer and dragged Brian outside.

Brian wiped down the table and cleaned off the four matching wooden chairs and Jenny slid a grey check tablecloth onto the table.

A few minutes later Sylvia carried out the casserole and vegetables on a large tray and they all sat at the table.

Brian looked at the empty chair. 'Where's, Jamie?'

'I told you he's out with his friends,' shrieked Jenny. 'I'm starving . . . you know what school dinners are like . . . Can we start now?'

They heard the back gate click open and Sammy, their golden retriever, hurtled towards the table and jumped excitedly up at Brian. Brian stroked him firmly and Sammy looked up at him expectantly. Brian and Sylvia had bought the dog soon after Jenny was born and were told by the breeder that he had been born on the same day as their daughter.

Jamie walked in and immediately sat down at the table.

Brian scowled at him. 'You're late!'

Jamie grunted and made to reach for his food.

'Jamie, you haven't washed your hands!' said Sylvia.

'Oh, mum . . .' he pleaded.

'Jamie, go and wash your hands,' said Brian.

Jamie made to stand but sat back down at the table.

'It'll only take a minute!' said Brian sternly.

Jamie stomped off towards the kitchen.

Brian served the food and Jamie soon rejoined them.

'What have you been up to today then, Jamie?' asked Brian.

'Out with me mates,' he mumbled. 'We went up to the old quarry'. He turned his attention towards the chicken casserole and stabbed at it with his fork. 'I'm starving'.

'Didn't you have any homework to do?' asked Brian tactfully.

'No, I didn't,' snapped Jamie.

'I hope you've been sensible and not doing anything dangerous,' asked Sylvia.

'Oh, come on, mum, I'm not stupid,' he replied.

'You are sometimes,' said Jenny.

'You be quiet, Jenny! What do you know?' he replied harshly.

'Come on you two, that's enough,' said Brian.

Brian looked at his family around the table and reflected on the day.

As soon as the meal was finished Jamie went to his room while Jenny chased Sammy tirelessly around the garden.

'What a lovely evening,' said Brian as he stroked Sylvia's shoulder. 'Hope we can do it again before the winter sets in'.

Sylvia turned around and suddenly looked sad. 'So do I,' she said. 'You've worked so hard to build up the company . . .' She stopped to watch Jenny chasing Sammy around the garden. 'And now we've got everything we ever wanted'.

Brian finished his wine and nodded. His mind elsewhere, he stood and collected the plates and walked towards the kitchen.

Sylvia turned away and wiped the tears from her eyes.

CHAPTER FIVE

All time low

As Brian drove into the company car park the latest single by *the Wanted* faded out on his car radio. 'Here is the seven o'clock news,' said the newsreader. 'It has been reported the British economy is likely to perform worse than any other economy in the western world . . .'

Brian mumbled to himself, reached forward and hit out at the on-off button on the car radio.

He unlocked the office, picked up the post and carried it through the eerily quiet building. He stopped for a few seconds and listened to the silence before he walked up the stairs and into his office. Today he felt more desperate and stood on the other side of his desk as he ripped the envelopes open instead of using his favourite letter opener. The brass letter opener, inlaid with two blue marble fish, swimming in opposite directions, had been a present from Sylvia when they started the business. Brian had always considered *Pisces*, Sylvia's star sign, to be his lucky charm. Much to his relief there were a number of large cheques and he totalled them on his calculator.

Jackie knocked on the door.

'Come in!' shouted Brian.

'You're in early today,' said Jackie.

'I know. I didn't sleep very well last night,' said Brian.

'You and me both,' replied Jackie.

Brian smiled.

'Yesterday's phone calls did a bit of good'. He looked down at the calculator. 'We've got over thirty grand to bank today'.

'Plus . . .' Jackie smiled. 'Pam said we should get Hanson's well overdue cheque tomorrow,' she said crossing her fingers.

'I'm just waiting for Harry to get in before I phone the bank. I want to speak to him personally'.

'Course,' said Jackie. 'Coffee?'

'Please'.

He shouted after her. 'Do you know what, Jackie? I reckon we're going to be all right . . . I have good feeling about today'.

Brian looked at the clock and checked it against his watch. He paced around the office, stopping briefly to tidy the magazines beneath the coffee table and moved the vase of flowers several times around his desk before putting it back in exactly the same position.

At exactly nine thirty he called the bank.

'It's Brian Chapman; could I speak to Mr Simms please?'

'Just a moment,' replied the clerk.

'Morning, Brian, how are you?' asked Harry Simms.

'Well I feel a lot better this morning,' said Brian as he pushed himself deep into his chair. 'To be honest I don't want another day like yesterday in a hurry. Jackie's on her way over to pay in a little over thirty thousand'.

'That is a relief, Brian,' said Harry his voice fading.

'Harry, are you still there?' asked Brian.

'Yes, Brian. I'm still here'. He paused once more. 'I'm sorry, Brian but I had to refer those two cheques to drawer'.

'What!'

'Bank policy, Brian. I'm sorry; it was taken out of my hands'.

'Fuck!' screamed Brian as he slammed down the receiver. 'The bastard!'

Brian tapped his fingers uncontrollably on the desk and called the tax office.

'Good morning, could I speak to Mrs Woodward please . . . It's Brian Chapman from BCPS'.

He continued to drum his fingers on the desk until he was connected.

'Mrs Woodward speaking, how may I help you?'

'Yes, good morning, Mrs Woodward, it's Brian Chapman. It's a courtesy call to tell you that the bank will be returning our cheque'.

He noticed the sharp intake of breath.

'No, there's no problem, I've just spoken to our bank manager and if you could represent it as soon as you receive it, it will be honoured immediately'.

'Thank you very much for letting us know, Mr Chapman . . .' She paused. 'Unfortunately our Department Head will need to investigate—'

'But . . . you will have your money tomorrow,' he pleaded.

'I'm sorry. Good day, Mr Chapman'.

Jackie knocked on Brian's door. 'I've paid them in . . .' She said as she tried to catch her breath. 'Thirty thousand, two hundred and sixty four pounds'. She smiled. 'What a relief?'

Brian couldn't share her enthusiasm.

Jackie couldn't help but notice the concern on Brian's face.

'I've just spoken to the VAT and tax office'.

'Was it all right?'

He suddenly looked confused and bewildered. He finally shook his head and thumped his desk.

'It's not! Harry, the *bastard* sent them back . . . both of 'em!' he screamed.

His mobile phone rang.

'I'll leave you to it,' she mouthed.

'Good morning, Brian Chapman'.

'Good morning, Mr Chapman, it's Nicholas Henley'.

'Morning,' replied Brian.

'I believe you may have need of my services?'

'Yes, I do,' replied Brian. He nervously drummed his fingers on his desk. 'Can you help?"

'I can't promise anything but David seems to think I may be able to do something to help. What's the shortfall?'

'About three hundred thousand,' lied Brian nervously.

'Mmm . . . What's the current turnover?' he asked.

Brian thought for a minute before replying. 'Last year?'

'The most recent you have please'.

Brian paused and screwed up his face as he thought. 'A few hundred shy of about two million'.

'Is that a few hundred or thousands?'

'Excuse me?'

'Is it hundreds . . . or thousands?'

'Ah, sorry,' said Brian, annoyed at his ignorance. He knew he would have to do better if he was likely to pull any deal off. 'We did a little over one point nine million,' said Brian.

'Uh, uh . . . Well . . . if the figures are correct then it may be possible . . . Can you email me through some details?'

'I've already completed figures for the bank,' gushed Brian excitedly.

'That'll be fine. Get them through to me this morning and I'll get back to you tomorrow'.

'Thank you, Mr Henley, good bye'.

Brian sat back in his chair and took a very deep breath before speaking. 'Fucking hell,' he said as he shook with a mixture of fear and apprehension.

CHAPTER SIX

Silence is golden

Brian and Sylvia sat in silence and watched the final minutes of an indie film but as soon as the credits rolled Sylvia jumped out of her armchair. Sammy pushed himself tighter into Brian's legs as his master's gaze remained fixed on the screen.

'It makes a change for us both to watch something together. I enjoyed that . . . didn't you?' she asked.

Brian turned to face her, his mind clearly elsewhere. 'Yeah . . . it was . . . it was good,' he lied.

'Fancy a cup of tea?'

'Go on then . . . why not'.

The screen flashed and the familiar ident for the late night BBC news broke the silence and they both looked at the screen.

'Good evening, here is the ten o'clock news,' said the newsreader. 'The headlines tonight . . . The recession is biting harder, three thousand jobs have been lost today and another hundred companies have been identified as being in financial difficulties and the CBI are threatening there is more bad news to come.'

'Did you hear that, Brian?' asked Sylvia.

She waited for a response. There wasn't one and she continued. 'Surely it can't get any worse?' quizzed Sylvia.

Brian reached out, flicked the remote and turned off the television. 'Where the hell is it going to end?' he said reaching for the brandy bottle. 'How can I even attempt to be positive when I go and see Harry tomorrow with news like that?'

'We'll be all right, won't we?' asked Sylvia.

'I don't know'. Brian shook his head. 'I just don't know'.

'Do you want me to come with you, Brian?' asked Sylvia.

Brian emptied his glass in one gulp and his reply spewed out. 'Well . . . it won't hurt, after all, you are a Director and I expect Harry would like to see you there'. He drained the last drops of brandy from his glass. 'Yeah . . . come . . .'

Sylvia began to shake and squeezed her hands tightly together to hide her anxiety.

Inwardly she wished she had Brian's resolve.

Brian walked into the noisy 'ops' office. Craig Jameson and a handful of the engineers looked up at him and the office suddenly fell silent.

'Morning, Brian,' they said in unison.

'I heard the video's going well,' said Craig.

'Yeah, it looked really impressive earlier this week,' said Brian looking up at the weekly job board.

'Do you think we'll all be film stars, Brian,' asked Jim.

Brian chuckled. 'You never know . . . a lot of the top film stars started like you'.

'How's work going, Craig?' he asked.

'Not bad actually. We've had a few jobs in already today and the first order from the Southbourne Building Society'. He smiled. 'I'm going to put Colin on that one'.

Brian fired him an angry look.

'Colin?'

Colin was taken aback and lowered his head.

'What's wrong with that?' he replied cockily. 'I plan the work . . .'

He stopped and looked directly at Brian. 'I'm the Manager . . . it's my job . . .'

'This is a new client . . . *what the hell were you thinking?*' screamed Brian.

Craig glared back at him.

'If you want to run everything . . . then you do it . . .' he said raising his voice.

Brian's face reddened with anger.

'Put Jim on that one and I want to see you up in my office in ten!'

Brian looked across at Colin Corke and forced a smile.

'It's not that I'm questioning your abilities, Colin but it's too soon to put you into a new client'. He coughed. 'You need a bit more time on the processes . . . right?'

Colin nodded his agreement.

Brian turned back to Craig.

'Ten minutes . . . my office!'

Brian first met Craig Jameson two years earlier. Craig, a little under six feet tall, blonde curly hair and a thin blonde moustache had walked into his office in 2008 looking for a job and the two of them immediately hit it off. They spent the next few hours talking about Brian's ideas and whilst Craig didn't have a trade he was able to carry out most maintenance tasks and Brian felt he would be an ideal person to work with him to grow the business. Brian had long since realised that Craig was only interested in himself and found it necessary to keep him continually under close scrutiny having suspected him of using the men and company materials for private jobs. Despite Brian's exhaustive efforts he had not been able to prove it.

Brian was talking on the telephone when the door opened and Craig rushed in. Brian ignored him and continued to speak. He finished the conversation with a smile and as he looked up at Craig his expression suddenly changed. Every line on Brian's tired face was exaggerated by his anger.

Craig didn't wait for Brian to speak.

'Brian, I'm the Manager what the hell did you think you were doing? You'll undermine my position with the men and then everything will go to pot . . . You know what they're like?'

Brian stared directly at Craig as he pulled subconsciously at his cheeks, shrugged and gave Craig a wry smile.

'What did you say . . . ?' He paused. 'I mean did you hear what *you* just said?'

Craig forced a smile.

'Course . . . I said I'm the Manager . . .'

Brian stood up and moved towards Craig stopping a few feet from him.

'*Manager!*' He screwed up his face in disgust, clenched his fists and as he raised them his whole body shook with rage. '*Fucking, Manager!* You're no more than a jumped up charge hand and don't you forget it!' He slammed both fists on his desk. 'When I say I want you to do something . . . You do it . . . No questions . . . *just do it!*'

He moved back to his desk, sat back in his chair and once more brought his hands down heavily onto his desk. 'Whose company is this?'

Craig's face reddened and he was lost for words.

Brian continued. 'Just remember that!' He lowered his voice and glared at him. 'And . . . if you dare to talk back to me like that again in front of *my* men—'

The telephone rang on Brian's desk and he ignored it.

'Get the *fuck* out of my office . . . and remember what I said!'

Craig stormed out of Brain's office and slammed the door behind him.

Brian picked up the phone and answered with a smile in his voice.

'Hello, Brian Chapman'.

Brian finished the call and sat on the edge of his desk as he slit open the last letter.

'Bloody hell,' he screamed.

Jackie looked apprehensive as she entered his office. 'Morning, Brian how is it?' she asked.

'Well . . . it was fine until I opened this one,' he lied as he passed it to her.

Jackie read aloud. 'In view of the default on payment of the VAT and Tax, Mr Edwards and Mr Williams will be visiting you on Tuesday.' Jackie looked at him. 'That's this afternoon?' She looked at his blank face. 'After the bank,' she exclaimed.

'And the radio interview,' said Brian.

She stopped and looked at him and tilted her head to one side before she continued. 'To discuss the overdue payment in greater detail—'

Jackie looked across at Brian and swallowed hard before she continued. 'At that time we will ask you how you intend to settle the outstanding amounts and to review any assets including vehicles and equipment owned by the company.'

Brian sighed and shook his head. 'I know, but at least we're seeing Harry first, so I will have *some* answers and I should hear from Nicholas Henley any time now'.

'Let's hope so, Brian'.

Jackie placed the letter on his desk, face down and covered it with the torn envelopes.

'Do you want a coffee?'

'Yes please . . . black'.

Brian's mobile phone rang. 'Good morning, Brian Chapman'. Brian nodded enthusiastically. 'Morning Nick . . . yeah I'm fine'.

'I've had a look through your figures . . . crunched some numbers . . . and think I may be able to help you,' said Nick Henley.

'That's really good news and . . . dare I say . . . great timing,' gushed Brian.

'Yeah . . . it's not been easy but I've taken the liberty of arranging meetings in London with investors I've used in the past'.

'When?' asked Brian impatiently.

'This Friday?' replied Nick Henley.

'That's no problem . . . the sooner the better. I'm seeing the bank this morning and I've got a visit by the VAT inspector this afternoon'. He sipped at his coffee. 'The bloody bank bounced their cheque'.

Nicholas didn't comment. 'See you on Friday at Docklands . . . I'll email details. Oh . . . and Brian, bring whatever you've got that might help your case and try and bring a rough cut of the video, we need all the information we can get and remember . . . positive . . . positive . . . positive'.

'Thanks Nick. I'll do what I can. See you on Friday'.

Brian let out a huge sigh of relief.

Brian and Sylvia walked into the Business Banking reception. Large posters covered much of the wall space offering to finance local and regional companies by lending them money. Brian looked at them and cursed under his breath.

The receptionist checked her computer screen and looked up. 'Good morning, Mr and Mrs Chapman. Mr Simms is running a little late but he shouldn't be too long. Please take a seat'.

Brian picked up the Financial Times, read the headlines, shook his head, scoffed and threw it onto the table.

The door opened and a shabbily dressed, middle aged woman limped up to the receptionist.

'Good morning, Mrs Wilson, can I help you?' asked the receptionist.

'Yes I hope so, dear,' she said nervously, her hands trembling. 'I've sold one of me horses,' said the woman.

'For how much, Mrs Wilson?' the receptionist asked sternly.

'A hundred and thirty five pounds,' she said, handing the cheque to the receptionist.

'I see,' said the receptionist.

'Can I write out a cheque from me account now?' she asked. 'I desperately need to get feed for the rest of 'em'.

'If you could hold on a moment, Mrs Wilson I'll have a word with the Assistant Manager'.

The receptionist pressed a button on her phone.

'Hi, Andy, I've got Mrs Wilson here in reception with me. She's brought in a cheque for a hundred and thirty five'. She carefully looked the cheque over before continuing. 'Yeah . . . it looks fine'. The woman turned and smiled nervously to Brian and Sylvie. With a look of disdain the receptionist eyed Mrs

Wilson across the desk. 'Mrs Wilson would like to issue a cheque?'

She placed her hand over the receiver and nodded.

'Mrs Wilson, may I ask how much it's for?' she asked.

'Fif . . . fifty pounds,' stuttered Mrs Wilson. 'I need feed for me 'orses . . . I gotta feed 'em, dearie,' she said.

She looked across at Brian and Sylvie once more and forced another smile but this time her desperation caused her to shake.

They smiled back.

'Fifty pounds . . . for horse feed,' said the receptionist before nodding to the invisible person on the other end of the phone. 'Fifty . . . that's right,' she repeated.

She replaced the receiver and took an extended breath.

'I'm sorry, Mrs Wilson but in the circumstances we can't allow you to issue any more cheques until this one clears—'

'How long with that be then?' she murmured.

The receptionist looked at the calendar. 'Next week . . . Tuesday at the earli—'

'They'll be dead by then!' she screamed. 'They'll be dead!' Mrs Wilson wrung her hands and with her head bowed she limped out of the office and wiped at the tears with her sleeve.

While the receptionist, clearly affected by the conversation, shook her head, Brian and Sylvia looked at each other in shock and sheer disbelief.

Sylvia fought to control her emotions and trembled nervously.

Brian noticed, squeezed her hand and whispered to her. 'Don't worry, love. They've got to support *us*'.

The door opened and Harry Simms, a very grey man, in his late fifties, wearing an equally grey suit, stepped out and shook their hands. 'Morning, Sylvia, Brian, please come in'.

They followed Harry into his office and Brian handed him the completed forms.

The bank manager took his time to read each page and frequently nodded as he turned the forms until he finally spoke. 'Well, it's as I expected . . . you've obviously realised that there's a shortfall of some two hundred thousand . . . and that's without these,' he said as he held up a handful of cheques that Brian had signed a few days earlier.

'That's right, Harry,' said Brian. 'But we are looking at the possibility of obtaining external funding . . .' he gushed. 'I have meetings in London on Friday'.

'Good'. He nodded slowly, deep in thought. 'But you will of course consult with us on any developments?' his expression suddenly changed and he waited for a reaction.

Brian nodded, looked across at Sylvia and smiled.

Harry continued. 'Before concluding any arrangements?' he asked sternly.

Brian's face drained of all colour.

Harry Simms turned to face Sylvia. 'Well, that's all well and good, but Sylvia, do you realise how serious this really is?' He waited for her reaction.

There was none.

He continued. 'I must remind you that you did give personal guarantees when we agreed the last facility . . . and we have a second charge on your family home'.

Sylvia began to tremble. 'What's that got to do with this?' she asked.

Brian reached for Sylvia's hand patted it gently, leaned forward and spoke. 'Harry, that's fine but you know all family companies make the same commitments and I'm sure *we* can get through this. We've nearly completed the company video and orders are still coming in. Our problem is cash flow'. He stopped and took a deep breath. 'If we can get our large clients to pay between thirty and forty days we would turn those figures around immediately'.

'But, Brian, they're *not* paying you are they?' said Harry shaking his head.

'They *are* . . . but slowly. I don't know what else we can do to speed them up. Could we not transfer our current overdraft into a long term loan . . . say over . . . ten years? That way we can spread the repayments and when we're out of this bloody 'credit crunch' we'll be able to pay off more of the borrowing?'

Harry screwed up his face and shook his head. 'You've heard the news, banks are hit as well this time around and we just haven't got the cash'. He paused and looked directly at Sylvia.

She moved uncomfortably in her chair.

'Six months ago you may have been able to do that but now.' He signed the deepest sigh. 'I'm getting a lot of pressure from Region'.

'Couldn't we arrange a meeting with them?' asked Brian.

Harry replied sternly. 'No. I'm afraid not. Things of that nature are generally left with me'.

Brian couldn't hide his anger. 'If that's the case, surely you can allow us a higher overdraft?' He looked hard at Harry and waited. There was no response so he continued. 'Because *you* didn't hold those cheques . . . as we agreed I've now got the bloody VAT inspector in this afternoon'.

'We didn't agree anything of the sort, Brian'. Harry shook his head wildly. 'And *you* know it!'

Harry ignored Brian's reaction and looked at directly at Sylvia while he continued. 'I couldn't,' he said.

She nodded her understanding.

Harry continued. 'You know I haven't got that many years left'. He scratched his balding head. 'And I don't want to jeopardise my pension'. His expression suddenly changed and he didn't hide his contempt as he spoke directly to Brian. 'Why the hell should I do that for *you?*'

Brian was shocked at the response and lowered his voice. 'Alright, Harry. So what's the answer?'

Harry stroked his chin with his pale heavily veined hand. 'Well, I've spoken to Region,' he said softly.

Brian squeezed Sylvia's hand hard in anticipation but as Harry continued he released his grip. 'They want an independent auditor to visit you as soon as possible; to check the figures and give us a report on how they see the business now . . . and where it may be in a year or two'.

Brian almost choked with shock.

'Harry! What do you mean by that? David and Richard are Chartered Accountants! The figures they've given you since we started the business are as accurate as anyone else could produce and you know that!' Brian flexed his muscles and exhaled heavily before he stood up. 'Come on . . . where's this leading, Harry?' He didn't wait for a reply but paced around the office before he turned to lean on Harry's desk.

The bank manager pushed himself deep into his chair. 'That's as maybe, Brian but if you want me to get you any more support, then I'm going to need this . . . and quick'.

Brian gasped and sat down.

'And who pays, Harry?'

'It's down to you, Brian,' he replied. 'You want the money . . .' He stopped to think. 'In fact . . .' He picked up the forms and pushed them towards Brian. 'You *need* the money'.

'That's ludicrous!' screamed Brian. 'One minute you're

telling me we've reached our limit . . . and the next . . .' He shook his head wildly. 'You tell me I've got to pay out even more cash . . . I don't have . . . to prove to you . . . and *whoever* . . . that the figures prepared by our company accountants are legit. It's crazy!'

Harry coughed loudly and looked directly at Sylvia and then Brian before he continued. 'And . . .' He paused once more and glared at Brian.

Brian and Sylvia both looked at him and waited for him to continue.

'. . . region also want a current valuation of your offices'.

Brian looked at him and thought for a second before he replied quietly. 'I can arrange that'.

'No . . . we'll use one of *our* approved surveyors,' said Harry.

'Are they clients of *this* bank?' asked Brian.

'Yes . . . they are,' replied Harry sternly.

Brian smirked.

'And the auditors?' asked Brian.

Harry nodded.

'How many other *clients* of the bank are earning from these totally unnecessary charges, Harry?' questioned Brian.

Harry sucked his bottom lip. 'I'm only following procedures, Brian'.

Brian's head dropped. 'You'd better get on with it then . . . set it up for any day next week,' he said reluctantly.

'That's fine, Brian'.

Harry Simms turned to Sylvia. 'Good to see you again,' he said before turning to Brian. 'By the way . . .' He gave Brian a callous look. 'In the meantime . . .' He paused and lowered his voice. 'Don't write out any more cheques'.

Harry reached across his desk and tapped his computer

keyboard. 'I see you paid in just over thirty thousand yesterday so, if you ask the Customs & Excise and Inland Revenue to represent their cheques I'll put them through for you'.

Brian looked at him the frustration and anger clear in his voice. 'That's fine now! But *you* created the problem for me!'

'Well,' replied Harry as he eyed Brian purposefully before he stood up. 'Brian, you know how it is,' he said as he forced a smile.

While Harry shook Sylvia's hand Brian stormed out of the office.

As they walked to the car Sylvia began to shake uncontrollably and broke down. 'What are we going to do?' she asked, choking back her tears. 'We're going to lose the house aren't we?' She took a huge breath. 'Brian, why didn't you tell me it was as bad as this?'

Brian shook his head wildly.

'Harry had to say that. That's the way they work,' said Brian, as he flicked the key fob. 'Shock tactics . . . they just want us to crumble'. He started the car. 'We won't though . . . we've worked too hard for that'.

Sylvia wiped her tears. 'Can you drop me home, please, Brian? I need some time on my own.'

CHAPTER SEVEN

Trains and boats and planes

'Welcome back. Our guest in the studio this lunchtime is Brian Chapman a local businessman who seems to be riding out what is without doubt the worst recession for two or possibly three decades.'

The music faded up and then down.

'Good afternoon, Brian it's good to have you back with us once more'.

'Good afternoon, Steve'.

'Tell me, Brian, what's your secret?'

Brian laughed. 'I'm not sure if there is a secret. We work hard and give the clients what they want'.

'That sounds easy enough . . . but what about getting paid for it?' asked the presenter.

Brian laughed. 'That is a problem and I make no secret of it . . . lately things have changed and every day we're finding it harder to get in the cash'. He paused. 'But so far we've been lucky,' lied Brian.

'I'm going to play some music and we'll be right back,' said the DJ, pushing the faders to play *the Flood*, the latest track by the reformed, *Take That*.

Off air Steve spoke to Brian. 'Thanks for coming in, it really is getting bad out there, we're losing advertising revenue like I can't remember'.

The on air light came on and the track faded. 'In the studio today, we have Brian Chapman, a local company director who is out there fighting the 'credit crunch'. Tell me Brian, do you think banks could do more to help business in general?'

'No question of that, Steve, I've spent the last two hours trying to convince our bank to do more but for some reason they either don't want to help . . . or can't'.

'Really,' said Steve.

Brian sucked in air before he replied. 'Yeah . . . I do. I feel there is an underlying problem that has still got to come out . . . it is certainly going to affect all of us in one way or another . . . As they say, watch this space'.

'That's interesting, I'm sure our listeners will have something to say about that. Thanks for coming in, Brian and I hope to see you again very soon. Thank you'.

Steve faded up the music.

'Thank you, Brian, entertaining as always. Let me know if there are any developments and we'll do the same next month. Thanks for coming in'.

Jackie walked into Brian's office carrying a coffee. She smiled at him. 'We heard the interview . . . sounded great as always . . . you've got a good voice for radio'.

Brian nodded his appreciation.

She passed him his coffee. 'How did it go at the bank?' she asked.

'Not too bad,' lied Brian. 'Harry wants to bring in an independent auditor to check our figure and projections and get the office valued'.

'Who pays for that?'

'We do, of course'.

'That's ridiculous'.

'That's exactly what I said to Harry'.

'Pam's got details of the meetings in London with Mr Henley on Friday. You need to be up and away early'. She stopped in mid-sentence. 'Are you going on the train or driving up?'

He answered immediately. 'Train.' He paused. 'Oh . . . and Pam, could you call the director at the video company and ask him for a couple of rough cuts of the DVD. Can you also copy up the forms I took to the bank, any press releases and cash projections we've got, I need to take them with me . . . four sets of each'. He looked at the wall. 'And four copies of the company photo,' he said.

Jackie unhooked the frame from the wall and left just as the phone rang on Brian's desk.

'Yes, Pam?'

'The gentlemen are here about the VAT,' she said.

'What, already?' he said.

'It is three o'clock . . .'

Brian looked up at the clock. 'So it is. All right, could you bring them up?' He sighed. 'I'll see them in the meeting room'.

The meeting room was functional, walls painted in the standard magnolia and white ceiling. At one end of the room was a flip chart, projector, television and video and in the centre four tables that could be arranged in many ways to suit the need.

Pam entered with two middle aged men wearing ill-fitting grey creased suits.

They stepped forward and shook hands with Brian.

'Good afternoon, I'm Mr Edwards and this is Mr Williams'.

Brian smiled nervously.

'Gentlemen, please sit down'.

'Well, Mr Chapman,' said Mr Edwards.

He removed the cheques from his battered brown briefcase. 'You know why we're here?' he said as he laid the cheques on the table in front of him.

Brian nodded.

'Your bank returned these cheques . . .' He tapped them gently. '. . . and asked us to refer them to drawer'.

Brian nodded again. 'U . . . uh,' he muttered.

'Mr Chapman, it's a very serious matter to issue cheques without sufficient funds to honour them'.

Brian spluttered defensively. 'I did call your office—'

'That is correct and it was appreciated,' said Mr Edwards. He cleared his throat. 'However, as a result of your call my supervisor asked me to visit you and discuss any underlying problems you may have with your business'.

For the first time Brian was able to relax and he smiled at them. 'Thank goodness for that,' he said softly. He sat back into his chair and laid his hands on the table. 'I told our bank manager that we were expecting quite a large sum of money this week, but he wouldn't listen'.

Mr Williams remained silent and nodded his understanding.

Brian continued. 'In actual fact the morning after I'd spoken to him we received more than enough to honour both your cheques'. Brian fidgeted. 'If you could represent them, I assure you that they will clear without any further problems,' he said proudly.

Mr Edwards continued. 'That's all very well, Mr Chapman and we will of course do that, but you do realise that you will be charged interest on the whole amount for the last quarter of VAT and as I understand it this month's National Insurance contributions and Income Tax?'

Brian made to stand but sat back in the chair. 'But that's ridiculous!'

Mr Williams nodded slowly.

Mr Edwards continued. 'I don't disagree with you, Mr Chapman . . . but rules are rules'.

Brian sighed. 'Well . . . if that's the way it has to be'.

'We're sorry about that but . . .' He gave him a stern look. 'You do agree to it?'

'Yes,' sighed Brian.

Brian watched as Mr Edwards removed a file from his briefcase, opened it and removed several forms and checked them before he continued. 'Unfortunately, we will need to have a signed guarantee from you regarding the next quarter's payment or we will hand things over to the bailiffs'. He turned and pointed towards the older man. 'Mr Williams and his colleagues'.

Mr Williams opened his day book. Brian looked across at him but turned his attention back to Mr Edwards.

'And next months tax, National Insurance and of course the last quarter of VAT,' said Mr Edwards.

Brian's face turned ashen. 'What do you mean, bailiff's?' he asked.

Mr Williams spoke for the first time. 'It means, Mr Chapman, that if you fail to pay your next VAT and Tax in full I will return with my colleagues and remove certain items. May I suggest we base this on, say six of your company vehicles?' He paused. 'I assume you own some of your vehicles?'

He waited for Brian to respond.

Brian nodded slowly.

Mr Williams continued. 'And any large items of plant, machinery and office equipment you own'.

'How is that, Mr Chapman?' asked Mr Williams.

Brian stuttered. 'W . . . well . . . yes,' he said, his voice failing.

'Fine'. He smiled. 'So we now need proof of any of your owned assets and we will list them on a *"walking possession order."* Could you please choose the vehicles and let us have sight of the log books and proof of ownership'.

Mr Williams turned to a new page of in his day book, reached for his pen and alternated between the book and forms.

Brian stood up. 'Yes . . . yes of course'. He picked up the telephone and dialled. 'Hi Jackie, could you please bring up the log books and plant file'. He nodded an answer to her question. 'Please . . . it's all right . . . No . . . I'll explain later'.

A few minutes later Jackie entered with the various files.

'Thank you, Jackie, this is Mr Edwards from the HMRC and Mr Williams . . .' Brian gave her a cagey look. 'He's . . . a bailiff,' he said guardedly.

Jackie was horrified. 'Bailiff,' she mouthed.

'It's fine,' he forced a reassuring smile. 'You may as well stay now you're here,' said Brian as he handed the files across to his visitors.

Jackie continued to stand at the door and watched the two men as they collectively deliberated over the log books and wrote down the relevant information.

Mr Edwards spoke directly to Jackie and smiled for the first time. 'Don't worry. Mr Chapman has explained everything and we'll be sure to represent the cheques tomorrow,' he said. 'Please take a seat.'

Jackie nodded nervously and finally sat down.

Brian smiled across at her.

'If it's any consolation, this is the fifth call today and you are the *only* company able to honour your returns,' said Mr Edwards.

'If you could please sign here and here and, Miss . . . if you could sign as a witness,' he said as he handed the pen to Brian and then Jackie.

The two men looked at each other and placed their respective books in their briefcases.

They both nodded with satisfaction and stood.

'Thank you very much, Mr Chapman . . . Miss, let's hope we don't have to meet each other again,' said the bailiff.

'Brian reached out and shook their hands. 'I'll agree with that,' said Brian.

Brian and Jackie watched them walk down the stairs and waited until the men left the building.

'Thank God for that,' said Brian, wiping the sweat from his forehead.

Jackie looked at him and mouthed. 'Coffee?'

'Please . . . black,' replied Brian.

'Can I tell Pam what's happened?' asked Jackie.

Brian didn't reply to her question but looked directly at her. 'Coffee?'

'Course,' said Jackie as she rushed out of his office.

CHAPTER EIGHT

Rescue me

Brian spent the whole journey reading and rereading the reports and going over every section of the figures and by the time he arrived at Docklands he felt very confident. The taxi pulled up outside a prestigious office block in Canary Wharf and he climbed out, paid the driver, straightened his tie, tugged at his jacket and walked in. Nick Henley was talking to the male receptionist and seemed intuitively to know it was Brian as he entered. He walked confidently towards Brian and as he shook his hand looked him up and down. 'Brian?'

Brian nodded.

'Nick Henley, it's a pleasure to meet you,' he said as he reached out to shake his hand.

Nick Henley, in his mid-thirties, was incredibly good looking with cropped blonde hair and wore a Gucci grey silk suit, handmade Italian shoes and an open necked dark blue striped shirt.

Nick led Brian towards the lift. 'Good journey? Did you bring everything?' he asked as they walked.

Brian nodded confidently.

'I hope you're on top form,' he said.

'We'll see,' replied Brian nervously. 'And I managed to get a rough cut of the video,' he said grinning.

Nick nodded and smiled. 'Excellent, excellent,' he said.

An hour later the lift doors opened and Brian and Nick walked out into reception and across the marble floored foyer. 'How do you think it went?' asked Brian nervously.

Nick smiled and patted Brian on the shoulder. 'It went very well,' he said. He paused and smiled widely. '. . . and Brian . . . I'm pleased to tell you that you've passed your apprenticeship'.

Brian looked at him quizzically. 'What do you mean?'

'Now you're ready to meet a real pro,' he said with a wide grin.

The two of them walked out of the lift on the tenth floor into the plush reception and Nick smiled at the immaculately dressed receptionist. 'Good morning. Mr Chapman and Mr Henley to see, Mr Jackman,' said Nick with a smile.

'Yes, certainly, Mr Henley,' she said before she turned, smiled at Brian and nodded. 'Mr Chapman, would you like to take a seat,' she said pointing at the thick dark brown Chesterfield leather settees surrounded by what seemed like a jungle of thick lush green plants.

Brian suddenly felt very nervous and couldn't sit down. Instead he stood looking at the huge photographs on the wall as the adrenalin pulsed through his veins.

Brian whispered to Nick. 'What did you mean back there,' he asked.

Nick laughed loudly.

'Listen Brian, did you really expect me to take someone I didn't know into a meeting without seeing for myself if they could handle the pressure?'

Brian wiped his forehead and licked his dry lips.

'No, I don't suppose you would,' he replied, feeling embarrassed at asking the question.

'How did I do?' he asked. But before Nick could answer him the telephone rang on the receptionist's desk. She picked it up and looked across at Brian and Nick.

'Mr Jackman will see you now,' she said.

She stood and led them down a wide corridor, knocked lightly on the full height hardwood door, opened it and they followed her in.

The office was sumptuous, fully glazed windows on two sides with patio doors leading onto a huge roof garden. One wall was covered in photographs of Mr Jackman with prominent business leaders, royalty and politicians.

Mr Jackman, a middle-aged man dressed in a dark hand stitched suit and bow tie stood erect and confident. He reached out and shook their hands firmly before he motioned to them to sit at a table away from his desk.

The subtle aroma of expensive freshly ground coffee beans wafted towards them.

'Good morning, gentlemen. Pleased to meet you, Mr Chapman. Mr Henley has told me a lot about you and your company'.

Brian looked out across Docklands and shuddered. *Had he finally made it?*

Mr Jackman continued. 'May I say it does seem very impressive?'

He poured each of them a coffee.

'Cream . . . sugar?'

Brian nodded for both.

Nick Henley shook his head. 'Black for me, please'.

Mr Jackman continued. 'I always like to meet my clients. Raising finance is an extremely specialised business and if I am to recommend the involvement of any of our clients I have to be sure that the business is suitable for their port-folio'.

Brian sipped at this coffee before speaking. 'Of course,' he replied nervously.

'If we do decide to participate in your company I would put together a deal and take 40% equity in your company, a seat on the board for one of our members as well as *close* involvement with yourself'.

He looked hard at Brian and waited for a response.

There was none.

'How does that sound to you?' he asked. 'After all this is *your* business and if we do manage to put a deal together things will never be the same'. He smiled broadly. 'I'm sure Nick has already explained that to you?'

Brian nodded and nervously edged the forms he had completed for the bank across the wide desk and waited nervously while Mr Jackman flicked through them.

Without any prior warning Mr Jackman suddenly stood.

'Well gentlemen, please leave it with me for twenty four hours and we'll come back to you'. He paused and looked directly at Brian. 'I assume we contact, Mr Henley?'

Brian looked back at him non-plussed.

'That's right,' replied Nick.

He led them to the door and opened it.

'Thank you very much, Mr Chapman, Nick'.

They shook hands and left.

Brian and Nick stood in silence as the lift glided silently to the ground floor foyer. A very relieved Brian was the first to speak. 'That didn't take too long did it? I felt very nervous in there,' he said.

'I don't blame you, Brian. You're dealing with one of the high flyers. Jackman's put together some huge deals lately and he's one of the few people who is still operating and not worrying too much about the recession and what's going on at the moment' He smiled. 'If anyone can help you, he can'.

Brian nodded in agreement but showed signs of apprehension.

Nick reached out to shake his hand. 'Brian, would you mind if I left you now? I have other appointments and I'm sure you will want to get back to your office today'.

Brian looked surprised.

Nick Henley laughed.

'I know what you're thinking,' he said

'Um . . .' muttered Brian as he nodded twice.

Nick Henley continued. 'Let me explain. If I had hawked your company around to these people . . .' He raised his right arm and, pointing it at the high rise offices that surrounded them, as he swung around three hundred and sixty degrees. 'Believe me . . . *they* would have smelt *desperation*'. He shook his head and smiled. 'And there would have been no chance of a deal'.

Brian recovered quickly and hid his disappointment. 'I understand . . . I'm sure you know best'. He looked at his watch. 'It's the Bank Holiday weekend and if I get back now I can tie up a few loose ends at the office'.

Nick Henley placed his hand on Brian's shoulder before speaking. 'Oh, and Brian, don't worry. I'll let you know as soon as I hear anything'. He paused and his face lit up. 'And yes . . .' He tapped Brian on the shoulder. 'Jackman does work weekends . . . Bye'.

They shook hands and went their separate ways.

CHAPTER NINE

What a wonderful world

Brian and Sylvia walked along the forest path and held hands while Jenny rushed ahead chasing Sammy through the heather and ferns. 'Isn't it beautiful here, Brian?' said Sylvia. 'Do you remember . . . we used to come here most weekends when we were first married?'

Brian reminisced. 'Even in the winter . . . We didn't seem to feel the cold then'.

'We must try and do it more often,' said Sylvia. She paused and spoke her thoughts out loud. 'I know times are very difficult but it will do us both good to get away from the office . . . and it doesn't cost us a penny to come up here'.

Brian squeezed her hand.

Jenny raced towards them.

'Come on, daddy, can you run with us? Can we go through there?' she said pointing at the thickest part of the forest.

Brian smiled. 'Go on you two,' he shouted. He turned to Sylvia before chasing after Jenny. 'Sylve, I'll meet you at the obelisk'.

Sammy raced ahead and Brian grabbed Jenny's hand and chased after him.

Sylvia stood watching until they disappeared into the forest and then made her way along the path. Tears filled her eyes and unable to hold back any longer she sobbed deeply. She loved the forest but today the tall dark trees blocked out the sunlight and everything seemed to be closing in on her.

Pam was stamping the post when Brian walked in. 'Morning, Brian . . . good weekend?

He ignored her question.

'Morning, Pam. Have you finished?'

She looked at Brian nervously. She wanted to hold back.

'I don't know if you'll like it,' she said nervously.

Brian's face suddenly changed.

'Well, what is it?' he asked impatiently.

She took a deep breath. 'Adams, Taylor and Partners want to come tomorrow . . .' She paused. '. . . to carry out the *audit*.'

Brian shrugged his shoulders. 'Well, what have we got to lose? The sooner the better . . . then we can put two fingers up to Harry and his sodding bank'.

Brian smiled at her.

'I tell you what . . . why don't we all go out for a meal tonight?'

A shocked Pam looked at him. *Socialising was something they only did at Christmas.*

'Yeah . . . why not,' she said.

Brian sat behind his desk opposite Mr Allan Taylor, the auditor. 'Well, Mr Chapman, we've completed the audit and agree with your Accountant's figures'.

Brian nodded with satisfaction.

'However, whilst I concur with your accountants that you need a two hundred thousand injection of capital and, although you hope to obtain it from outside investors, there is still an immediate shortfall of some seventy thousand pounds. As I see it, you have two options; either you obtain payment from some of your major clients within the next few days'. He lowered his voice and for an instant became sympathetic towards Brian. 'Perhaps offer an incentive discount for prompt payment, or obtain the amount from another source'.

Brian looked at him and tried to take in what he had just said. 'What do you mean, I need it immediately?'

'Well, you know the bank won't support you any further and I feel that if you are able to raise some of that yourself, then the Bank might decide, and I am stressing might . . . decide to allow you a slightly larger facility'.

He took his time to look around Brian's office. 'There is of course, another option,' he lowered his voice. 'Off the record, this business could go into administration, or you could liquidate it, then you could find a buyer to take the business on'.

Brian looked at him stunned and confused. 'But I don't know anyone who could do that,' he replied.

Allan Taylor smiled at Brian. 'I do,' he said.

'Who?' asked Brian as he screwed up his face in total shock.

'*You* could buy it,' said Mr Taylor.

'Me? Where do I get the money? You just said we need seventy thousand'. He shook his head. 'Like now?'

'I can't answer that for you, Mr Chapman'.

He slipped the file into his bulging flight case and stood up.

'So . . . can I ask when your report will be with the Bank?' asked Brian.

'Well, normally in circumstances like this I'd go away and prepare my report . . . but in this instance, I'll come back tomorrow, late afternoon. If you are in agreement with the contents, as Directors, you and your wife will need to sign it and I will present it to the Bank. However, if there are any amendments then I will correct them and then present it'.

Brian looked relieved. 'Fine . . . thank you very much'.

Brian parked his car outside the unassuming pre-war terraced house, looked up, and sighed before pushing the unlocked front door gently and walked into the kitchen.

'Hello, mum,' said Brian.

'Hello, Brian nice to see you, what a lovely surprise,' replied Mrs Chapman.

Mrs Chapman was a tiny woman, in her late seventies. She had been a widow for more than twenty years and had lived in the same terraced house since she married Brian's father immediately after the war.

'Cuppa tea?' she asked.

'Please, mum,' replied Brian, as he sat at the dining table.

Brian gazed at the kitchen wall, above the now redundant fireplace, completely covered with framed photographs of him in his first school uniform and more recent photographs of Jenny and Jamie in almost identical poses.

'I haven't seen you, Sylvia or Jenny for a few weeks now . . . and . . . as for Jamie, well . . . I think it was last Christmas'.

Brian unhooked a photo from the wall, sat at the table and stared at it intently.

'So what's the matter? I only seem to see you these days

when there's something wrong,' asked his mother as she filled the kettle.

'Sorry, mum, I've had a few problems'.

Mrs Chapman looked concerned. 'I always thought you came to me when you had problems?' she said sternly.

Brian managed to force a smile. 'I do, mum, but this is different—'

She fired questions at him without taking a breath. 'What on earth is it? You're not ill are you, son? Problems with Sylvia . . . Jenny?'

'Course not . . . not even with Jamie'. He smiled. 'And you know what teenagers are like?'

She nodded and joined him at the dining table.

'Well, what then? Come on, son, what's going on?' she asked clearly agitated.

'It's the business. The banks are not playing ball and we're having all sorts of problems trying to get money from our clients'.

'Not those supermarkets and superstores?' she fumed.

'Yeah . . . some of them,' he said.

'Well, if that's the case I'll stop shopping at May's,' she said.

Brian laughed. 'That won't help, mum, they're huge . . . they don't care about us'. His finger traced the faces on the photograph. 'We're just one of many. Other companies are beating their doors down to work for them'. He sighed. 'If only they knew'.

The kettle boiled and switched itself off.

'Come on, Brian, out with it?'

'I've just had people in to look at the books—'

'And what did they say?'

'They've said it's a great business—'

'Course it is, son,' she nodded erratically, 'course it is,' she said proudly.

'That's fine . . . but what they said is . . .' He subconsciously traced the pattern on the table cloth. 'I need to raise seventy thousand now while I wait for the outside investment . . . and the guy who I was with today reckoned that if I can put in some of that . . .' he stopped himself.

'Well?'

'Well, then the bank might let me have a little bit more'.

'What's stopping you? Why don't you?' she asked enthusiastically.

'Where do I get that sort of money? We've remortgaged the house and the bank has a second charge on it . . .' He sighed. '. . . as well as the overdrafts'.

He placed the photograph on the table.

'There's nowhere else I can try,' he said, shaking his head and unable to hide his feeling of defeat.

His mother stood up switched the kettle back on, waited until it boiled and poured the water into the teapot.

'There you are. We'll have a nice cup of tea'. She looked at him and smiled the broadest of smiles. 'I've got some of your favourite biscuits,' she said as she opened a tin and took out a new packet of chocolate digestives.

'Thanks mum,' said Brian with a smile. He started to open the biscuits but then looked across to her. 'Don't things ever get you down?'

'At my age I reckon I've seen most things and one thing is for sure . . . you only have one life and we should all make the best of it'.

Mrs Chapman sipped at her tea and stopped suddenly. 'Brian, I've got an idea,' she said. 'I haven't got a mortgage.

This house if paid for . . .' She smiled excitedly. 'Couldn't I borrow money against it and lend it to you?'

'Um . . . I suppose you could . . . but how would I pay it back?' asked Brian.

'I wouldn't worry about that . . . we've had some good times in this house and you're going to get it eventually anyway, so why not have some of it a bit earlier? Eh . . . ? What do you think?' she gushed.

His mother took the biscuits from him, opened the packet and passed them to him.

'Well, I suppose you could maybe take out a short term loan against the house and then I can pay it back when things pick up'.

Mrs Chapman couldn't hide her excitement.

'There you are then'.

She refilled the kettle and switched it on.

'All right, mum, I'll have a word with David, my accountant, in the morning and see if he can arrange a loan. I do appreciate this, mum'.

'That's what mum's are for . . .' She busied herself washing the dishes before she turned to him. 'More tea?'

'Yes please, mum. That could save us'.

He ate three more biscuits.

Jackie sat in her car and dialled her mobile. 'Hello, Sylvia, it's Jackie'. She waited for a reply. There was none and she continued. 'How are you?

Sylvia finally answered her. 'Fine . . .' she muttered. 'I'm fine'.

Sylvia had been crying and Jackie could sense the anxiety in her voice.

Sylvia collected her thoughts and continued. 'How are you?'

'I'm fine,' replied Jackie brightly. 'Just thought I'd give you a call to see how Brian's coping?'

'What do you mean?' replied Sylvia obviously shocked.

Jackie thought hard before she replied. 'Well we've all been finding it hard lately, what with the VAT . . . the bank, and people chasing for money on a daily basis. It is a bit wearing'.

Sylvia finally realised what Jackie had said. 'Brian's all right isn't he?' she asked apprehensively. 'I mean he seems to be coping really well. Um . . . he told me he'll have things sorted out any day now'.

Jackie forced a smile before she spoke. 'Of course he will. Brian always comes through'. She stopped abruptly. 'Well Sylvia if you fancy going out for a girly drink and a chat give me a ring. OK?'

'Thanks, Jackie that will be nice . . . Bye'.

Sylvia replaced the receiver and broke down once more.

Brian stood in David Thornton's office and waited apprehensively while he finished his telephone conversation. He replaced the receiver and smiled.

'Well, Brian, it's good of your mother to allow you to do this. Are you sure she understands the implications?' he asked.

'I'm not sure she totally understands everything, David, but I've got to get over this somehow . . . and it does look good with Nick and the London investors'.

David nodded. 'Yes, I've spoken to him and he seems optimistic. Mr Jackman was very impressed and I believe it takes a lot for him to back things at the moment'.

'Can you prepare the papers?

'I'll get right on to it, Brian'.

'Thanks, David . . . now I've off to see Harry, the banker'. He paused and smiled. 'Yeah . . . I did say banker'.

CHAPTER TEN

Silk degrees

The curtains blew in the warm evening breeze, casting a combination of shadows and flashes of streetlight across the bed. The bedroom floor was strewn with the couple's clothes, empty champagne bottles and broken glass. On the modern sideboard was a part used line of cocaine and collection of empty aromatherapy oil bottles. The man gyrated and thrust his tanned pelvis while the woman writhed between the twisted dark blue silk sheets. She let out yells of pleasure until the sexual combatants reached a climax and slumped exhausted into the mattress. As they lay quietly the woman stroked Craig's well-formed muscular and hairy chest and twisted the hair slowly between her fingers.

Craig lit a joint and the woman gently rubbed aromatherapy oil into his skin.

'That was fantastic,' she purred.

Craig accepted the complement and smiled. He took a long drag from his 'special' cigarette before he spoke. 'Yeah, I know,' he bragged. He took an even deeper drag and closed his eyes.

The woman stroked his chest and continued to twist the long blonde hairs between her fingers and tug them. 'Craig, do you know this is our second anniversary?'

'Yeah, I know,' he replied smugly.

'Craig . . .' she asked.

He ignored her.

She continued. 'Why can't we do this more often?' she asked.

Craig took a huge drag on his cigarette before he spoke. 'If we can get this shit over with, Brian . . . perhaps we can—'

'It will . . . It's only a matter of time . . .' She stopped briefly. 'Trust me'.

Craig pushed her arm aside and rolled out of bed He tore back the curtains and stood looking out into the night, his toned and oiled body glistened in the street light.

The woman jumped out of bed and joined him at the window and her hands explored every inch of his body.

'Craig?'

'Yeah?'

'Will you ever leave your wife?'

'Why should I do that?'

The woman moved away from him and pulled on her silk dressing gown.

She turned. 'What if I had money?' She paused and waited. 'What would you say then?'

He turned to her. 'Perhaps . . .' He smiled at her. 'You never know'.

She gave him the widest grin and turned away.

'I'm hungry . . . come on,' he said as he pulled on his shirt.

Brian waited impatiently while Harry Simms read the auditor's report. He played with a broken nail flicking at it nervously.

Harry looked up and for once, his face had what appeared to be a genuine smile. 'I'm pleased to see the report from Adams, Taylor and Partners bears out what you and your accountants have told us. As a result, I feel we can increase your overdraft facility by a further seventy thousand pounds, providing you can arrange a similar amount, and . . . you continue to push your clients to pay'. He paused and Brian waited expectantly. It didn't take long and Harry's face was suddenly transformed into the sullen grey appearance that Brian had recently come to know. 'All that of course is subject to Region's agreement . . . and your signature on the new forms'.

Brian's euphoria was short lived.

'What forms?' he asked.

'Well, Brian, Region have asked me to arrange for you to sign these'. He passed the forms across to Brian. 'Basically they are assurances from yourself, that should the company go into administration, you will assist the liquidators and that the seventy thousand pounds . . .' He paused and looked closely at Brian as he continued. 'Providing of course you can match that amount'.

Brian nodded slowly.

Harry grimaced and continued. 'I must tell you that your amount will not be repaid, until we, the bank, has received payment in full of all monies loaned to you including the overdraft amount . . .' He paused. 'Plus of course interest'.

He waited for Brian's reaction.

'Do I have a choice?' asked Brian.

Harry Simms tapped his desk and looked up at the clock. 'In all honesty, Brian, I don't think you do but I must place on record that I am not forcing you to sign these'. He pointed to the forms on his desk. 'However, unless you do so, we can't help you any further'.

Brian pulled the pen from his pocket, reached across, scanned the forms and signed them.

Harry Simms countersigned them and handed Brian a copy.

Brian drove back to his office in silence. He was confused because on one hand he seemed to have averted losing the business but on another he was now deeper in debt with the bank but until he heard from Nick Henley he had no alternative. 'Pam, could you arrange for all the office staff to be in here for a meeting at four o'clock this afternoon,' he said. 'And, I want all the men here as well. Ask Craig to arrange that please'.

'Sure, Brian, I'll get on it right away'.

All the staff waited nervously in the general office. There was an air of fear and anticipation, but no one really knew what to expect. Brian walked in and stood near the door. He looked unusually serious. 'Thanks for coming,' he said.

Some of them nodded, some of them stared blankly at him while others lowered their heads.

'I've called you in this afternoon because I want to make you all aware of our current situation. The Bank is giving us a lot of grief so we are now looking at raising funds elsewhere'. He looked slowly around at each of them but there was still no reaction. 'There's a great chance that we'll be able to raise the large amount of money we need to stay in business. In the meantime, I've been able to borrow more money and the bank has also agreed to increase our overdraft. All I can ask is that we try to save money wherever we can'. Once again he looked around at everyone before he continued. 'And if we all pull together I'm sure we'll get through'.

The atmosphere became a little more relaxed and everyone present smiled with relief.

'Are there any questions?' asked Brian.

There were none.

The engineers left the office in silence and walked out into the car park.

As soon as they were out of the office the mood suddenly changed.

'I told you we were in trouble,' said Jerry sarcastically.

'What do you expect . . . look at the money he's spending on the poxy video,' said Richard.

'Yeah, look at the car he drives. He just wants to be flash. He doesn't give a damn about us,' said Johnny.

They climbed into their vans and revved their engines, tyres screeching as they raced out of the car park.

Brian sat in his office and watched the engineers as they raced the company vans around the car park before chasing each other out onto the road. He shook his head in disgust and muttered to himself and as the sense of despair engulfed him he covered his face with his hands.

Jackie suddenly burst into his office. He slowly parted his hands and looked across at her.

In the euphoria of the moment and failing to notice his mood she spurted forth. 'Brian, we've just had this email from, Mr Henley!' Jackie said excitedly shaking it in front of her.

He sighed, rubbed his hands vigorously across his face and reached out for it. 'Let's have a look,' he asked.

She passed it to him and stood over him while Brian slowly read it. His face initially lit up as he read the first page but as he began to read the second page his expression reverted to a look of disappointment.

'Have you read this, Jackie?'

'Yes, Brian, I have,' she replied somewhat subdued. 'I brought it straight up . . . I *thought* it was *important*,' she said stressing every word.

'Yes, Jackie, it is,' said Brian as he read and reread the front page. Without looking up he continued. 'Nick says that Mr Jackman is prepared to help us'.

'That's great news, Brian . . . really good news'.

She rushed around his desk reached over and hugged him tightly. She relished every second before she moved away.

'Well it is'. He said as he threaded the paper between his fingers but Jackman wants fifteen thousand up front and Nick has asked for an advance of five thousand, to cover his costs and introductions fee'.

'It's catch 22, isn't it?' said Jackie.

Brian took a huge breath before he exhaled slowly.

'It is'. He shook his head and forced a smile. 'Let me read it through again . . .' He paused as he scanned the bottom of the front sheet. 'Um . . . You'd better bring up the cheque book'.

Brian reread the email again and shouted after Jackie.

'Jackman doesn't want a cheque . . . he wants a bankers draft'.

Brian picked up the phone and dialled.

'Hi, David, I don't know if you've heard anything but I've just heard from Nick . . . Nick Henley. Jackman has agreed to take us on'.

'That's good news, Brian. I had an email earlier from Nick

but I didn't want to tell you . . .' He paused. 'I wanted you to get the good news from him yourself'.

'David, did you know they want like . . . twenty grand between them before we even start? Is it safe?'

'Well, Brian, all I can tell you is they both have impeccable references and excellent reputations . . . but it has to be your decision'.

'And what a decision . . . twenty fucking grand?'

Brian replaced the phone and flicked furiously between his calculator and note pad before he picked up the phone once more and hit a couple of buttons.

'Jackie, could you please call Harry Simms and ask him to raise a bankers draft in favour of Mr Jackman's Company for fifteen thousand pounds and I'll need a cheque for Nick Henley'.

He replaced and receiver kicked hard at the floor and pushed himself away from his desk.

CHAPTER ELEVEN

Paint it black

Jackie, her face ashen with shock replaced the telephone and looked across to Pam. 'What the hell was that about?' asked Pam. 'It looks like you've seen a ghost.' Pam laughed loudly. 'Or won the lottery . . .'

Jackie looked at her.

The printer on Jackie's desk ground into action and spewed out an email. Jackie picked it up and read it. 'It's not funny . . .' She bit her lip hard until it bled. 'How the hell can I tell, Brian?'

Pam got up from her desk.

'What the fuck has happened? Come on . . . out with it Jackie!' she screamed.

Jackie picked up the email and read it to Pam.

They both sat in deathly silence.

Pam and Jackie walked slowly up the stairs in silence.

Jackie knocked on Brian's door and they both remained at the threshold.

Brian was completing an estimate for a potential client and listened to a CD of *The Script*.

He looked up and smiled at Jackie but upon seeing Pam and

the shock on both of their faces he stood and walked slowly towards them.

'What's up?' he asked, his voice fading.

Jackie couldn't speak.

She blindly handed him the email. She so desperately wanted to hold him and protect him from the evil outside world but held back.

Brian read it twice and let it drop onto the carpet.

He fell into the settee and shook his head wildly as he screamed out. 'Fucking hell!'

He continued to repeat the same words until his voice faded and he gasped for air. 'How on earth can a company like that go bust?'

Jackie looked across at him, closed her eyes and threw her head back.

She wanted to cry but knew that would make things even worse.

'Pam, how much have we had in today?' growled Brian.

'Next to nothing, Brian,' she replied nervously.

Brian grabbed at the email pushed past them and left without saying a word.

Pam and Jackie looked at each other and shook their heads.

'The poor bastard,' said Jackie.

'I think it's much worse than that, Jackie,' said Pam.

Brian sat in front of David while he read and reread the single page. His concerned face further unnerving Brian. David looked up slowly and took a moment before he spoke. 'You've only banked sixty thousand in the last three weeks, plus your mother's loan and the bank's seventy. Is that right?'

Brian nodded and kicked at the threadbare carpet. 'Yeah . . .' He sighed. 'That's about it'.

'Well, Brian it looks like we've run out of options'.

'We!' screamed Brian interrupting his mentor.

David coughed and continued. 'I can only suggest one thing'.

'W . . . w . . . what the fuck is that then, David?' he stuttered.

'Liquidate the company,' he said softly.

'What!' Brian paused and tried to think. 'Isn't there anything else we can do?'

David sipped at his coffee and pondered. He reached for his calculator and tapped away feverishly. 'You said that you banked sixty. What are you owed at this precise moment?' He paused and studied Brian's face. He looked tired and exhausted, a man clearly overawed by the magnitude of the problems that were engulfing him. David coughed nervously and forced a smile.

Brian took the pad from David's desk and scribbled the larger debtor amounts before he raised his head. 'Well, assuming they all pay me'. He rechecked his figures. 'I reckon three hundred plus'.

'I'm not sure if there is anything I can do to help . . . leave it with me a couple of hours and I'll get back to you'.

He stood and tapped Brian's shoulder in an attempt to reassure him.

'Keep your cool . . . there may well be something we can do'.

Brian left David's office, his head bent and shoulders sloped. 'Thanks, David . . . I'll hear from you then?'

Pam and Jackie heard Brian's tyres screech as he skidded to a halt in the front visitor's car park. They sat bolt upright in their chairs and waited for Brian to walk in. 'Are you all right, Brian?' asked Pam.

He walked past them without speaking and took the stairs up to his office and slumped into his chair.

Almost immediately the phone on his desk rang breaking the unusual silence.

'Brian, its David for you,' said Jackie.

'Hi David'. He exhaled angrily. 'I tell you what; it's been like an eternity waiting for your call'.

'I know. It's never easy. I've spoken to an Insolvency Practitioner, Jonathan Thomas from Fischer and Hager, and he can get in this afternoon'.

Brian didn't answer.

'Well? Shall I arrange it?' asked David.

'OK, but I have got one more chance. I'm going to see someone I met at the club,' said Brian. He coughed and then continued. 'I haven't told him the whole situation yet but he's a merchant banker, I shouldn't be more than an hour so could you ask Jonathan to come in after four . . . let's keep it as low key as we can eh?'

Brian arrived back at his offices and without saying a word Jackie signalled to him and he raced up the stairs and into the meeting room. David and a smartly dressed stranger sat around the table and were busy discussing the company's financial situation when Brian entered. They both looked up at him and David stood and forced a reassuring smile.

'Brian, this is Jonathan Thomas from Fischer and Hager,' said David.

Brian shook Jonathan's hand.

'So how did it go?' asked David.

'A fucking waste of time, I'm afraid. If you've got a problem with one bank, it seems like you've got a problem with all of 'em,' cursed Brian.

'I think you're right, Brian,' said Jonathan. 'It's like the bush telegraph'. He sighed. 'Remember, they all know each other'.

'Let's get on with it,' said Brian.

Jonathan flicked through the papers before looking up. 'Brian, I see you put in seventy thousand a few weeks ago. That will be lost'. He said in a matter-of-fact tone. 'We'll do what we can about your house, but everything else . . .' He raised his arms and stretched them behind his head.

Brian pushed himself deep into his chair.

The door opened and Jackie walked followed by Sylvia.

Brian's whole body stiffened as he stood up.

'What's Sylvia doing here?' he shouted.

David stood and guided Sylvia into the room and sat her down.

'She's a Director, Brian. *All* Directors have to sign,' he said firmly.

Brian mouthed to her. 'Sorry'.

David sat beside Sylvia before speaking.

'Sylvia, you know I've acted for you and Brian for many years, and what we're going to have to do today has happened to so many companies . . .' He forced a half smile. 'You really mustn't take it personally. It's not for the want of trying on Brian's behalf,' he said.

Jonathan nodded his agreement and David followed suit before he turned back to Sylvia.

'Sylvia, Mr Thomas is an Insolvency Practitioner. He will do all he can to help and guide you through this. Rest assured . . . if you need any help, day or night, please call me . . .

and Sylvia, make sure Brian *does* call me'. He gave Sylvia a reassuring smile. 'You've got my mobile and home number?'

Sylvia couldn't speak but nodded slowly. She reached across and held Brian's hand.

Jonathan pulled a handful of forms from his flight case and while everyone sat in silence he filled in the details from the information David passed across to him. 'If you will both sign these, and . . .' He looked across the table. 'David, if you could witness them, I will speak to the bank in the morning. These papers allow us to act as liquidators for Brian Chapman Services Limited and I would think, knowing the way you've run the company, most of the details can be wrapped up within three or four weeks. You will of course need to dismiss all your office staff . . .' With his face devoid of any emotion he stared at Brian. 'And the whole of your workforce . . .' He paused and took a deep breath. 'And . . . I suggest that this is done first thing in the morning'.

Brian and Sylvia looked on in sheer disbelief unable to take in what was happening around them.

Jonathan reached into his case once again and handed Brian a letter.

'This is the letter that must be typed on headed paper, signed by one of you, and handed to everyone . . .'

Brian gazed blindly ahead.

Jonathan continued. 'And it will allow everyone to register at the Job Centre, claim any redundancy monies, and wages they're owed along with holiday pay'.

CHAPTER TWELVE

Turn back time

'The Prime Minister is assuring companies that the banks will immediately make more credit available to companies,' said the newsreader.

Brian switched off the car radio and hit the pre-programmed number for Harry Sims on his mobile phone.

'Hello, Brian'.

'Harry, what's this about banks lending to companies?

'Don't believe all you hear, Brian. You know they need as many votes as they can get . . . nothing more. Sorry, Brian—'

Brian cut Harry off before he'd finished.

Jackie sat at her computer and typed the dismissal letters and each time she typed a new name at the top of each letter she paused and reflected on the recent events before moving on to the next.

Brian walked into the office and she immediately grabbed his attention. 'Brian, have you heard the latest the news? They're saying that banks will be forced to lend money to companies!' she gushed excitedly.

'What do you reckon? Is it worth a try?' She looked at him expectantly and waited.

Brian looked at her, his eyes confused and tired.

'What they say is not what they *actually* mean . . .'

Brian left the office without saying another word.

Pam waited until she could hear Brian walking into his office before she gave Jackie a cunning look. 'I've been seeing someone for a while.' She smirked at her and bit her lip. 'And we have plans.' she said with an extended smile.

Jackie was genuinely surprised. 'Really . . . have you?' She looked at her quizzically. 'You never mentioned it before'.

'Well . . .' She frowned at Jackie. 'Why should I?' she said sharply.

Jackie blushed.

Pam continued. 'He lives in Plymouth'.

Jackie smiled at her. 'You're a bit of a dark horse aren't you, eh?'

Pam glared at her.

'Sorry Pam.' She rubbed her chin nervously. 'It just came as a shock . . . I've never heard you mention anyone. That's all . . .'

'Well?' replied Pam.

'I know . . . I'm just surprised you never mentioned it?' Jackie played nervously with her hair. 'Why on earth not?' she asked.

'Why should I?'

'Well . . . I just thought—'

Pam reflected. 'Dunno'. She walked across to her desk. 'Anyway, I've put some money away . . . so maybe I'll move to Plymouth and start my own business'.

Jackie was shocked at Pam's response and got up from behind her desk. 'What?'

Pam stroked at her hair. 'Well, I don't have a job here anymore so why not start somewhere else—'

'With him . . . I suppose?' asked Jackie.

Pam smiled coyly and blushed. 'Probably,' she said softly.

The staff stood in the general office and Brian entered, his face grey and haggard, deep lines across his forehead and dark pockets beneath his eyes. 'I'll keep this brief'. He paused and swallowed hard. 'I'm afraid we've run out of luck . . . and money'. He looked at the floor, took a huge breath and continued. 'Sylvia and I would like to thank you *all* for your hard work and help . . . especially over the last few difficult months. Last night we had a meeting with our financial advisers and, as Directors, we had no option but to liquidate the company'. Brian could feel a lump in his throat and he coughed nervously. He continued but his voice was almost inaudible. 'Th . . . th . . .' He coughed hard and started again. 'Thank you everybody'. He turned to Jackie. 'Jackie has your dismissal letters . . . you'll need to take them to the Job Centre. Any money you're due will be sorted out by the liquidators as quickly as possible'.

There was total silence.

Brian, now pale faced and exhausted, sat awkwardly on the edge of Jackie's desk.

Everyone looked hopelessly around at each other.

Eric, a young trainee clerk, stepped forward and spoke directly to Brian.

'Brian . . . um . . . Mr Chapman, if there's anything I can do to help I'll work for nothing . . . I've really enjoyed it here,' he choked with emotion.

'So will I if you want me to,' said Jackie.

'And of course you can rely on me,' said Pam.

Craig Jameson scowled at Brian. 'It's alright talking about paying wages, but *when* are we going to get them?' he screamed.

Brian contorted face looked back at him.

Craig continued. 'I've got a family to support and two young kids! I can't go home and tell my wife that my wages will come through *some time!* When *am* I going to get *paid?*'

Jackie clenched her fists and shook with rage. 'Thank yourself lucky Brian's kept you on . . . you've certainly not been pulling *your* weight lately,' she said. 'You're a lazy sod!'

Craig stepped back and pushed his way through the group and stormed out of the building and raced away in his company car.

Brian sat at Craig's desk surrounded by all the engineers. They were crammed into an office too small for the number of men. 'You've probably all heard by now but me and Sylvia have got no option but to shut the business down,' he said quietly.

Brian could feel the unrest building up and saw the anger on some of their faces.

Harry was the first to speak out. 'Well . . . you can stuff your fuckin' van! I'm off . . . Come and get it if you want it!' he screamed.

Richard and Johnny spoke simultaneously. 'And mine!'

The three of them forced their way between their workmates and slammed the door behind them. They climbed into their vans, revved the engines and raced round and around the car park their tyres screeching.

Several more followed them and they all gathered in the car park.

Brian watched them through the window as they remonstrated with each other and vented their anger on the vans, kicking out at them and denting the doors and side panels.

Craig drove back into the car park and pulled up immediately outside the office. He jumped out of his car, leaving the door open and engine running. With a final act of bravado he steamed into the office and began to empty his desk drawers. He grabbed at his laptop, stapler, calculator and Dictaphone and anything else he could get his hands on.

Brian grabbed at Craig's arm, forced it behind his back, and twisted it forcefully.

'You know that's company property,' he snarled. 'You can't just take that!'

Ignoring the pain Craig continued to stare hard at him.

'You can have it back when I get my wages!' he seethed. Craig broke out of Brian's grasp and threw everything into a box and stormed out.

Everyone else left the office in silence leaving only the shocked Colin Corke.

Colin lowered his head and struggled to speak. 'I really thought I'd broken the jinx this time, Mr Chapman,' he said softly.

'I'm sorry it hasn't worked out, Colin . . . I did try,' sighed Brian.

Brian walked back into the general office with some of the outstanding jobs and files from Craig's office. Eric and Jackie tidied the files and ledgers but Pam jumped nervously when she saw him. 'Just sorting out a few files before they arrive tomorrow,' she nervously.

Brian didn't hear her.

'Did you really mean what you said?' he asked them.

They all nodded.

'I really appreciate it . . . you know that,' said Brian sadly.

'It's the least we can do, Mr Chapman,' said Eric proudly.

Brian squeezed his arm. 'Could you all come in tomorrow then?' he asked. 'There's no need to rush in, there's not a lot we can do and I'm waiting for a call from Jonathan Thomas. He'll have talked to the bank so we'll know what their reaction is soon'.

The phone rang and Jackie picked it up.

'Good afternoon, Brian Chapman Services. Can I help?' she asked and nodded as the caller spoke. 'Yes, that is correct, we *are* in liquidation'. The voice at the other end continued and Pam who was nearest to Jackie could hear every word the caller shouted. She shook her head in disgust. 'The bastard,' she mouthed.

Jackie continued. 'I really don't know what the situation is. We've only just heard ourselves but we have appointed the liquidators and I know they will sort everything out'.

She replaced the receiver and shook violently. 'My God, it doesn't take long for bad news to travel, I wonder who told them?' she asked.

Early the next morning Brian sat at his desk. There was an incredible stillness as he shuffled his papers before screwing up the superfluous pages and throwing them into the already overflowing waste bin. There was a knock at the door, it opened and in walked Jonathan Thomas. Brian looked towards him, his face drawn and his eyes bloodshot. 'Hi Jonathan, I've been waiting to hear from you. Have you spoken to the bank?' he asked.

'Yes, I have. They're refusing to accept our appointment,' said Jonathan.

'Can they do that?'

Jonathan screwed up his face. 'I'm afraid they can,' he said. 'If I know them, they'll want to appoint, Adams, Taylor and Partners'.

'But . . .' Brian looked confused. 'They're the company who carried out the audit'.

Jonathan pulled a face. 'It's incestuous isn't it? Do you see now how these banks work?'

Brian opened a small cabinet between the two settees, poured two glasses of whiskey and handed one to Jonathan.

'Thanks, Brian. Have you dismissed everyone?'

Brian nodded.

'Good. Then I suggest you all go to the Job Centre'. He looked directly at Brian. 'And that includes *you* and *Sylvia*'.

'What?' asked Brian.

'Well if you take my advice, you ought to do that. You're owed your salary and holiday pay as well as redundancy. If you don't register, you won't get any of that'.

'How can I be paid redundancy? It's my business,' asked a bewildered Brian.

'You're still an employee, aren't you?'

'Well, I suppose I am. I pay tax and National Insurance'. He reflected. 'Yeah . . .' He shook his head rapidly. 'Why not?'

Jonathan took a final swig from his glass and emptied it. He studied the empty glass before he placed it carefully on Brian's desk. 'There you go, get what you can . . .' He smiled. 'From what I've seen of your business you've certainly earned it.'

He reached out, shook Brian's hand and left.

Brian spent the next few hours backing up all the company information onto an external hard drive and memory stick while he tidied his desk.

CHAPTER THIRTEEN

Help me make it through the night

When Brian returned home Jenny was in her pyjamas and dressing gown and Sylvia was brushing her hair. She looked up at him as he entered the room. 'Hello daddy. Look, Sammy's keeping my feet warm'.

Sammy was stretched across her feet, his tail wagging contentedly.

'Isn't he clever?' said Jenny.

Brian looked down at Sammy and feigned interest.

'Um . . . he's very clever,' he said half-heartedly.

He bent down and stroked the dog.

Sylvia could see Brian was overwhelmed – *a sad and broken man.*

He chewed at his nails.

'Go on, Jenny, off you go to bed!' said Sylvia harshly.

'But mummy, daddy's only just come home . . . can't I stay up for a few more minutes?' She looked at Brian expectantly.

'Not tonight, darling,' he coaxed. 'Be a good girl'.

'Alright, mummy . . . daddy . . . Good night,' she said. She kissed her father and mother before grabbing her favourite doll and patting Sammy on the head.

'Nigh . . . night darling,' said Brian.

Sammy raced after her bounding up the stairs and into her room.

Sylvia put her arms around Brian's neck and squeezed him hard. 'Brian, what on earth are we going to do?' she asked softly.

Brian shook his head and fell into the arm chair. 'I don't know . . . I just don't know,' he said.

Sylvia broke down and started to cry uncontrollably.

Brian could feel the tears welling up inside him but managed to hold them back. The phone rang and he picked it up.

'Hello . . . hello . . . who is this?' he asked.

He listened to the silence before he slammed the phone down.

'Who was that, Brian?'

'I don't know . . . but whoever it was . . .' he looked at the phone '. . . was bloody offensive'.

'That's the fourth call tonight, Brian,' she trembled as she spoke. 'What *are* we going to do?' she said, her voice breaking with a combination of fear and anger.

'I really don't know, Sylv . . . I just don't know,' said Brian as he tried to hide his true feelings. 'I tell you what . . . I'll go and get a Chinese'.

Sylvia smiled at him. 'That *will* be nice,' she lied.

Brian pulled on his fleece but as he opened the front door he turned to her. 'Don't open the door to anyone'. He took a deep breath. 'I mean anyone!' he said sharply.

Sylvia nodded wildly in agreement.

He turned as he picked up the car keys. 'And . . . don't answer the phone. OK . . .'

Sylvia nodded. 'Don't be too long—'

'Course not,' he said.

He kissed her on the cheek and left.

Brian returned to find the house in darkness. He slipped his key in the front door and pushed it open apprehensively. He thought hard about switching on the hall light and decided not to do it. He whispered. 'Sylve . . . are you there?'

He heard a noise in the lounge. He dropped the takeaway bags onto the hall carpet and cautiously picked his way into the lounge. All he could see in the darkness was the LED display on the television and DVD console.

'Sylve . . . where are you?' he whispered.

Then it began.

The only light in the room disappeared as the power was cut.

His mobile phone flashed, buzzed and shuddered all at the same time on the coffee table.

The landline telephone rang out.

The front doorbell rang randomly.

There was frenetic knocking on the back door.

Gravel ricocheted off the lounge window sounding like a machine gun firing at them.

Sammy raced around the room barking and yapping uncontrollably

It was total mayhem.

It suddenly stopped as quickly as it had started.

There was now total silence.

Sammy raced upstairs, back into Jenny's room and onto her bed.

Sylvia crawled out from behind the settee. Brian slid along the floor to join her and held her tight. She trembled in his arms and struggled to breathe.

A scaffold tube crashed through the lounge window stopping a few inches from where Brian had been kneeling a split second earlier.

Shards of glass fell on top of them.

They lay motionless and waited.

The house was once again totally silent except for the refrigerator purring in the kitchen.

Sylvia reached out and picked up a piece of the broken glass and sipped it into her pocket before she suddenly snapped. 'What's happening to us?' She became hysterical and unable to hide her abject terror any longer screamed uncontrollably.

She ran out of the room and kicked out blindly at the takeaway bag on the hall floor scattering the contents onto the carpet and over the wall. She raced up the stairs and stood on the landing as she struggled to breathe. She shook her head wildly and banged it hard against the wall. Her irrational action caused her to lose her balance and she slipped on the top step and crashed down the stairs landing amongst the Chinese food.

Brian raced out to find her body twisted and distorted in the hall. 'What the f . . . !'

He bent over her and supported her head. 'Sylve, are you all right? Speak to me . . . come on . . . say something,' he urged.

Sylvia briefly opened her eyes before she coughed heavily and vomited onto him. She moved her head erratically and now in shock she mumbled incomprehensible gibberish.

Brian panicked, grabbed at the hall telephone and dialled 999.

While he gave them his address Sylvia felt inside her pocket, found the piece of glass and sliced deep into both of her wrists.

Brian turned back to her to see the blood pumping from her wrists. He threw down the phone and in a state of sheer panic rushed up the stairs. He returned almost immediately with a handful of towels and bound them around Sylvia's wrists.

'What the hell has happened to you?'

He pulled the towels tighter around her wrists.

'Did you do this?' he asked numbly.

Sylvia's traumatised eyes stared right through him.

Brian tried to console her but it had no effect and she continued to shake her head wildly and mumble incoherently at the door.

Within a few minutes there was a knock at the front door which quickly became a loud hammering.

Brian reached up and nervously opened the door wide enough to see who it was. When the flashing blue light raked across his face he opened the door a little wider.

The male paramedic cautiously pushed his head between the door and frame and flashed his ID card. 'Mr Chapman? You called 999?' he asked apprehensively.

Brian swung the door wide open, nodded frenetically and pointed to Sylvia.

The paramedic pulled a torch from his pocket before he entered followed by a female paramedic who appeared extremely wary of Brian. Her suspicions were based on the numerous cases of domestic violence she had witnessed over the years in her job.

The male paramedic spoke. 'Don't worry. We're here to help you now'. He forced a half smile. 'I'm Mark'. He pointed at the young woman behind him. 'And this is Julie'.

Julie forced a smile. 'Can you tell us what happened?' she asked.

Brian mumbled incoherently. 'I don't know,' his arms flailed around uncontrollably. 'She . . . Sylvia . . . her . . .' He took a huge breath before he continued to speak. 'We've been having a few problems . . .'

Julie pulled back anxiously and gave Mark a furtive look.

Brian leaned against the open door and swung it backwards and forwards. '. . . and I don't think she can handle it any more . . . Can't cope—'

'Alright,' said Mark nervously. 'Let's have a look, shall we?'

'Sylvia, can you hear me?' asked Mark.

Now in a catatonic state Sylvia burbled to herself.

They placed a mask on her face and administered oxygen before they removed the blood soaked towels from her wrists.

'We need to stop the bleeding,' said Mark.

Julie tied tourniquets above the deep wounds and pressed hard on the cuts. 'She's going to need stitches in here,' she said pointing at the cuts, 'and possibly a transfusion'.

Mark turned to Brian. 'Do you know your wife's blood group?'

Brian shook his head. 'Um . . . no. We've never been ill . . . Never,' he mumbled.

'Don't worry, Mr Chapman . . . we can take care of that,' said Mark.

The bleeding was staunched and Julie examined Sylvia for broken bones and surprisingly, with the exception of a few cuts and bruises on her arms and legs, she was uninjured.

They sat her up and propped her against the wall and then looked around at the congealed Chinese takeaway on the carpet and wallpaper.

Julie looked at the rice and food and screwed up her face. 'Do you have a couple more towels I can use to cover this up?'

Brian pointed up the stairs.

Julie pulled out her torch and squeezed past Sylvia. She returned a few minutes later with several large brightly coloured beach towels, which she placed on top of the food and wiped down the walls with a smaller towel before she threw it into the corner. 'That's better,' she said calmly.

Mark looked up at Brian quizzically.

'It's . . . *Brian* . . . Chapman isn't it?' he asked.

'Ye . . . as,' replied Brian guardedly.

'My brother, Colin used to work for you,' said Mark. He pondered for a moment and appeared genuinely upset. His voice faltered. '. . . very sad to hear what happened'.

Brian looked at him blankly.

Mark stopped and tilted his head to one side. 'To your business.'

'Colin?' asked Brian as he returned a blank look.

Mark continued. 'Colin Corke?'

'Ah . . . yeah . . . Colin . . . He only joined us a couple of months ago,' said Brian as his voice tailed off to a whisper.

Brian turned and looked forlornly down at Sylvia.

'Can you tell *me* what happened, Mrs Chapman?' asked Julie.

Sylvia partially lifted the mask and spoke slowly as she tried to explain that she had *fallen* down the stairs. But as she recalled the horror of the menacing phone calls and the scaffold tube being thrown through the window she became exceedingly agitated and let out a piercing yell. Her screams echoing up the stairwell.

Mark and Julie shot each other a knowing look.

Mark couldn't hide his concern and stood up.

'Could I speak to you, Mr Chapman?'

While Julie continued to treat Sylvia's cuts, Mark closed the front door and guided Brian into the lounge. 'Mr Chapman, I'm sorry to say this but we believe your wife is having a nervous breakdown'. He paused and shone his torch around the room. He noticed the scaffold tube and broken glass on the carpet and coughed. 'Things don't look too good'. He pointed at the broken glass. 'Do you think that has anything to do with it?'

Brian visibly affected by the recent events, broke down. He slumped onto the carpet and held his head in his hands and sobbed uncontrollably. He finally spoke through his fingers. 'What do *you* think? 'Course it has . . . but they don't give a shit about that,' his voiced faltered and faded.

Mark was clearly effected by Brian's outburst and the rapid decline in someone he had never met but his brother had told him so much about. Someone, Colin had told him was the most dynamic and positive person he had ever met or worked for.

Brian continued. 'Do they?' He suddenly shook his head wildly. 'No one gives a shit! No one!' he screamed as the desperation ate right through him.

The paramedic moved closer to Brian and spoke softly. 'I'm really sorry about all this. Shall I call the police?'

Brian wiped his nose with his sleeve and looked up at him. 'You're wasting your time . . . I know who's doing this and I'm sure the police do . . .' He sobbed again. 'They can do nothing . . . Nothing . . .' His voiced cracked with emotion. 'Nothing . . . no . . .'

Mark was looking at a defeated and helpless man.

'I'll see if I can get the lights back on shall I, Mr Chapman?' asked Mark.

Brian nodded.

The few minutes later the lights came on revealing the damage that had been caused in a few short seconds. Mark returned to the lounge, smiled and sat on the floor with Brian.

Julie called out. 'Can you come out for a minute please, Mark'.

Mark stood up and rubbed Brian caringly across his shoulder. 'I won't be a minute, Mr Chapman,' he said softly.

Mark stood in the doorway and watched Sylvia as she talked to herself in childlike gibberish and traced the patterns on the stained wallpaper with her index finger. Without saying a word Mark walked out to the ambulance and made a call on his radio. When he returned, he nodded to Julie, and walked back into the lounge and sat on the carpet next to Brian. 'Mr Chapman . . . Brian . . . I'm sorry to have to tell you this but we both feel your wife . . .' He paused. 'Sylvia . . . needs special treatment'.

Brian looked up at Mark through his distended bloodshot eyes. 'What? Special tr . . . tr . . .' his voice faded to a whisper.

'There's nothing to worry about,' said Mark.

He looked around the room and tried to take in as much as he could about his patients and their family. He was used to that and he could quickly form an opinion of who and what he was dealing with. Satisfied with his assumptions he returned his attention to Brian and continued. 'But it will be for the better . . . for both of you,' said Mark. He stroked Brian's head and lowered his voice to a whisper. 'It will . . . It really is for the best'.

Brian trembled.

Mark helped him onto the settee and wrapped a blanket around him. 'Now we've got the power back shall I make us all a cup of tea while we're waiting?'

There was no reply.

Mark returned a few minutes later and handed Brian a mug of weak tea loaded with several spoons of sugar. He pointed to the framed family photographs fixed symmetrically on one wall. 'Are those your children, Brian?' he asked as he pointed at the largest of the photographs.

Brian looked out over the rim of the mug and nodded.

Mark suddenly looked concerned. 'Are they in the house?' he probed.

Brian looked up at the photo they had been taken just six months earlier at a professional studio. 'No . . .' he said shaking his head half-heartedly.

'Ah,' said Mark thankfully.

Brian pointed to Jamie. 'Jamie's at Robert's for a few days.' He then pointed to his young daughter. 'Jenny . . .' He slurred. 'She's upstairs'.

'Upstairs?' Mark shot Brian a look of deep concern. 'Really . . . *She's* upstairs?' He took a moment to gather his thoughts. 'Oh . . . is there anyone who can look after her? Jenny? Tonight?' he asked.

Brian took a huge swig of tea and tried to concentrate. 'Well . . . she could stay with my mother'. He stopped abruptly. 'What time is it?'

Mark checked his watch against the decorative wooden clock on the opposite wall. 'One thirty,' he said clearly surprised at how long he and Julie had been at Brian's home.

He stood up. 'Give me your mother's number and I'll give

her a call'. He reached into his jacket pocket and pulled out his mobile.

Brian struggled to remember the numbers but as he gave them to Mark he carefully dialled each number.

The phone rang for several minutes before Mrs Chapman finally answered.

'Hello, who is this?' asked a very sleepy woman.

'Good evening, Mrs Chapman, my name's, Mark, I'm a paramedic'. He could hear the panic in her voice. 'No . . . no . . . there's nothing to be worry about but I'm here with Brian and Sylvia'.

She fired questions at him. 'What's happened? Is it Brian? Jamie? Is Jenny all right? What *has* happened?'

'No . . . it's nothing to worry about and everyone *is* fine . . .' He lowered his voice. 'There's been an accident and we need to take Sylvia to hospital for observation'.

Mrs Chapman continued to fire questions at him.

When she paused for a breath Mark spoke. 'It's OK . . . Really . . . she fell down the stairs—'

'Are you sure she's alright? I want to speak to my Brian!'

Mark passed his phone to Brian.

'Hello, mum. No . . . no . . .' He gasped for breath and continued. 'Don't worry, mum. No, Sylvie's OK, but she needs to go to hospital'.

'What!' she exclaimed. 'Hosp—'

Brian ignored her question. 'Can Jenny stay with you tonight and maybe tomorrow?'

'Course she can. Why did you even ask that, Brian? I'll get the room ready . . . you take care of yourself and . . . and give Sylvia my love'.

'Thanks mum . . . thanks'.

Mark took the phone from Brian and put it back into his pocket before he reached for his radio and made another call.

The doctor arrived a few minutes later. 'Good evening'. He coughed and corrected himself. 'Good morning, I'm Doctor Thompson'.

While Doctor Thompson examined Sylvia, Mark explained the situation to him. The doctor then turned his attention to Brian. He checked his blood pressure, temperature, chest, ears and lastly his eyes. 'You do need to get some rest now, Mr Chapman'. He said as he looked around the lounge. Clearly concerned at what he had seen. He sighed before he continued in a softer tone. 'Is there someone we can call for you?' he asked.

Brian gave the doctor a vacant look.

'To come over and stay with you?' asked the doctor.

Brian drawled. 'I don't think that will be necessary . . .' He took in a huge breath. 'It was just the shock . . . Things have been building up for a while now and tonight was . . .' He stopped suddenly and scratched frantically at his head his nails digging deep into his scalp.

The doctor reached out and gently pulled Brian's hands away.

Brian looked down at his bloody finger nails, wiped his eyes and continued. 'Tonight was?' He ran out of breath and took a huge gulp of air. 'Tonight was . . . the last straw . . .' He shook his head and looked around the room. 'I'm sure we'll be fine after a good night's sleep . . . something neither of us has had for . . . for months'.

The doctor sighed. 'Um . . .' He rubbed his chin while he thought. 'Well, Mr Chapman, I'm afraid I need to get your wife a little more than that. She needs *special* treatment'. He looked at Mark and then turned his attention to Brian. He continued in a low voice. 'She is clearly very distressed and we need to section her . . .' He paused anticipating some reaction from Brian but there was none. The doctor continued. 'It's the best for both of you'. He waited for Brian's reaction. Once again there was none. 'Are you happy with that?' The doctor moved nearer to Brian before he continued. 'Mr Chapman?'

Brian continued to stare at the wall, confused and bewildered.

'Mr Chapman . . . Mr Chapman . . .' asked the doctor.

Brian turned towards him and gazed at him blankly. 'Mr Chapman, I have one more question for you'.

Brian didn't reply.

The doctor moved closer to Brian and lowered his voice. 'May I ask if your wife is pregnant?'

Brian closed his eyes and shook his head erratically.

The doctor smiled at him. 'That's fine'. He nodded. 'If you have no objections I'll make a call and make the necessary arrangements'.

The doctor left the room with Mark and after he made his call he gave Sylvia an injection of Lorazepam. He sat down beside her and continued to check her pulse as the drug quickly took effect. He released her limp hand, took a form from his bag, filled it in and signed it. He waited a few more minutes and nodded to the paramedics. He passed the note to Mark and nodded towards the front door.

Julie and Mark lifted the sedated Sylvia into the carry chair, strapped her in and took her out to the ambulance.

The doctor returned to Brian, took a pad from his pocket, wrote an address and phone number on it, tore out the page and pushed it into his limp hand. 'You must get some sleep now, Mr Chapman . . . and don't worry . . . your wife is in safe hands'.

He tapped the note.

'Please call this number in the morning and you will be able to make arrangements to visit your wife'. He smiled reassuringly. 'It really is for the best,' he said softly.

A young woman walked through the open front door. She showed her ID card to Mark and he led her into the lounge.

The doctor immediately recognised her and smiled.

Mark guided the woman towards Brian and he knelt down in front of him.

'Brian, this is, Niki Simpson, she's from social services and she will be taking Jenny to your mother's tonight.'

There was no reaction from Brian.

'Brian, if you give us her address then Niki will take her?'

Brian suddenly became agitated and distressed. 'Will you take her to *my* mother's?' He glared at her. 'I mean . . . y . . . y . . . you're not taking her into *care* are you?'

Niki sat next to him on the settee. 'No, Mr Chapman . . . if there were no family members available to look after Jenny . . . then *we* would'. She smiled at him. 'We just need to be sure that's all.' She wasted a smile. 'Don't worry . . . we won't be involved after tonight'. She looked directly at him and continued in a firm voice. 'Unless of course . . . there *is* a problem'.

Brian looked to Mark for reassurance and mouthed the last word. 'Problem?'

Mark nodded to him and smiled. 'It will be fine,' he said softly. 'Don't worry . . .'

Brian sighed heavily. 'Alright,' he said. He tried to stand but began to shake with a combination of anger and hopelessness and muttered to himself. 'What a fucking mess?'

'Come on, Brian,' said Mark. 'Let me give you a hand'.

Mark helped Brian up from the settee and guided him gently up the stairs.

Brian entered Jenny's room and switched on her bedside light. Sammy was asleep at the foot of her bed. Knowing he was not allowed up stairs had chosen to ignore the visitors. Brian stroked him and he snuggled deeper into the duvet. Jenny was still sound asleep and Brian shook her gently to wake her up. He trembled as he spoke and tried desperately to hide his anguish. 'Jenny,' he said softly. 'Sorry, love but you need to go to your Nan's tonight . . . mummy's poorly'.

She didn't reply.

Jenny had always been a heavy sleeper and always slept through the loudest of Jamie's obscure metal music.

Niki helped her into her dressing gown and slippers while Mark selected clothes for the next morning and packed them neatly in a sports bag.

Niki carried a still sleeping Jenny downstairs and out to her car and threw the bag onto the back seat.

Mark helped Brian into bed and waited until he was comfortable.

'Your wife will be fine, Brian,' he reassured him. 'She *will*'.

The doctor followed them upstairs and after checking Brian's pulse passed him two tranquillisers and a glass of water. He continued to monitor Brian's pulse until he drifted into a deep sleep.

Mark pulled the duvet over his patient and pulled the curtains. 'Just give her a bit of time,' he said softly. 'Things will seem so much better in the morning'. He filled a small case with some of Sylvia's things and looked back at his sleeping patient.

Mark whispered to the doctor. 'Why him? It can't be right? Surely someone's to blame for this misery?'

Doctor Thompson shrugged and closed his bag.

Mark pushed the note deep into Brian's hand, switched off the light and closed the bedroom door.

CHAPTER FOURTEEN

Are you lonesome tonight

The heavy rain woke Brian. He reached out to Sammy who was snuggled deep in the duvet and fell back to sleep. A few hours later the late morning sun burnt through the clouds and slowly crossed the room. He still held the note from the doctor tightly in his hand as he pushed himself up and sat on the edge of the bed. He opened his eyes fully and immediately squinted as the sun caught his face full on. He shielded his eyes, lay back on the bed and gathered his thoughts. It was several minutes before the events of the previous night came back to him. He suddenly felt the note in his hand, jumped off the bed and dialled the number on the paper.

'Hello,' said the voice at the other end.

'Hello, who is that?' asked Brian.

'This is Gresham House'.

'Erm . . .' Brian was taken aback and had no idea what or where Gresham House was. He continued. 'This is Brian Chapman . . . I understand my wife . . . is with you?' he asked nervously.

'Who is this?' asked the voice at the other end of the phone.

'Sylvia Chapman . . . My wife should be with you . . .' he said angrily.

He waited while the person at the other end tapped at the keyboard.

'That is, Mr Chapman?' she asked.

'Yes, that's me . . . I'm Mr Chapman, her husband.'

'Ah. Well Mr Chapman. Yes, she is with us'. She paused and took a deep breath. 'It's best if you don't visit today'. She paused again and waited for Brian to speak but he didn't answer her. 'Mrs Chapman is fine and resting. We're keeping a close eye on her'.

'When can I come and see her?' gushed Brian.

'May I suggest we wait a couple of days?' said the voice.

'Erm . . .' He fiddled with the paper. 'So I can't even visit my *own* wife? Not even for a few minutes?' He shook violently as he raised his voice.

The voice at the other end of phone continued. 'We'll see you next Tuesday'. She paused. 'Please call us anytime, good bye'.

Brian replaced the receiver and looked around the room.

He talked to himself. 'Come on Brian get a grip. If *you* don't no one else will'.

He pulled on his tracksuit and went down to the kitchen, filled the kettle and switched it on.

Sammy raced excitedly around the lounge treading in the broken fragments of glass.

'Sammy! Keep away from this or you'll hurt yourself!' screamed Brian.

Sammy didn't understand but could tell by the tone of Brian's voice that he had to obey.

Brian cleaned up the glass and made the first of three calls.

'Hi, George sorry to trouble you on a Saturday but I need

the lounge window sorting out'. He nodded. 'Yes it's doubled glazed but I need it patching today . . . single glazed . . . yeah I know it'll be a couple of weeks for a new unit. Great!'

He made the second call.

'Yeah, I need a mortice lock on the front. Great!'

He made the third call.

'Hi, Sally. I need a favour'. He nodded as Sally replied. 'Today please'.

He made himself a coffee and walked out into the garden.

Sammy ran wildly around the garden for a few minutes. Until he realised he was hungry and he nuzzled Brian. Brian returned to the kitchen, filled Sammy's bowl, tore the 'TO DO' pad from the wall and walked back out to the garden.

He sat at the garden table and read the notes, details and appointments.

Sylvia, dentist Friday 9:30; Jenny, swimming lessons, Tuesday 5:00; Brian, order prescription 14th; Jamie trip to Alton Towers with Richard on the 18th; next month; renew car insurance and tax the car.

The list had everything on it; absolutely everything.

Sylvia was so well organised and for the first time Brian realised how much she had contributed to their marriage and family. While all he did was work.

He thought he knew everything.

He didn't and had forgotten how much Sylvia actually did.

The business was *his* life.

As he walked back into the kitchen he sipped at his coffee and thought hard about his life and what had gone wrong. Unconsciously he poked at the cards on the board and they dropped to the floor. It revealed Sylvia's favourite photograph of Brian fixed to the board with discoloured brittle sellotape.

He smiled to himself.

He thought. *I still have that.*

He left the mug on the worktop and walked into the garage. He moved the cases and boxes, tools and garden equipment before he uncovered the hard guitar case. He removed the acoustic guitar from the case and despite the strings being a little rusty he was able to tune it. He walked back into the garden and strummed and strummed until he found some chords he liked. While he played he recalled how he met Sylvia. He was playing at a wine bar in Clifton Bristol, where he was at college. She came in with a group of friends and after they left she stayed behind and chatted to him. He saw her the following week and within a month they were inseparable.

Why did he stop playing? He could have been a pro.

Love!

They married a few months later in 1989; Brian was 23 and Sylvia 22. He left college and with the opportunity to join a National Maintenance Company they moved to Devon where he began work as the assistant branch manager. Sylvia encouraged him to continue playing the guitar but his new job would soon take over much of his life and he left the once valued instrument under his bed until they moved into their new house where it was stored in the garage and left to gather dust.

Brian carefully put the guitar back in the case and stood it up against the lounge wall behind the settee.

As always, his mind returned to his business and he cursed to himself. 'They won't get away with this shit'.

He washed, showered and shaved and as soon as the window was repaired, the locks changed and the hall carpet and walls cleaned, he drove to his mother's.

Jenny and his mother were pleased to see him. Jenny raced

over and hugged Brian as though they had been separated for weeks.

'Cup of tea, son?' asked his mother.

'No thanks mum'.

She couldn't hide her disappointment.

His mother continued to stare at him, with a quizzical look on her face.

She waited. And waited.

Unable to hold her silence any longer she finally spoke. 'Well . . . ?'

Brian looked across at her. 'I thought we'd all go out for the day . . . have lunch and try to relax—'

'Relax?' she replied angrily.

Brian shrugged. 'You know what I mean?'

'Do I?'

His mother couldn't hide her anger.

He ignored her.

'Come on you girls . . .' he coaxed. 'Get your coats on'. He turned. 'Don't forget, Sammy!'

Sammy heard his name and raced out to the car and they waited until his mother reluctantly joined them.

They drove in silence except for Jenny's constant chatter in the back as she played with Sammy.

Brian's mother couldn't hold back any longer. 'Well, Brian is there *any* news of Sylvia?'

Brian failed to answer.

'Well, how is she? She is *your* wife,' she said harshly.

Jenny stopped playing with Sammy and waited for her father's response.

'She's alright. Yeah . . . she's fine. She'll be out soon,' his voice faded as he accelerated away.

CHAPTER FIFTEEN

Somebody help me

In 1842, the Metropolitan Commissioners in Lunacy reported on Collaton House, recommending that it increase the size of the building and its grounds for the patients. As a result, the Governors of Collaton House decided, that rather than extend the present institution, they would build a new facility to improve the treatment of their patients. Twenty acres of land was acquired on the headland at Shadford in Milton, east Devon, Mr West was employed as the architect, and the foundation stone laid on the 18th October 1866. The Earl of Devon opened the new 120 bed Gresham House on the 7th July 1869. The new building was large and airy, with a grand entrance accessed by a flight of sweeping granite steps. A billiard room was included for gentlemen and social spaces provided for the patients to mix. Doctor Shapter, the chronicler of the Milton cholera outbreak, already a physician at Collaton House, was appointed to manage the hospital.

More than a hundred and forty years since the building was first occupied Brian drove along the coast to the highest point on the headland and through the ever open heavy wrought iron ornate gates towards Gresham House. He turned into the private gravelled drive and saw the imposing Victorian Gothic building for the first time. He parked his car in the tight gravel car park and looked up at the once magnificent and ornate building, its lime stone walls weathered with years of sea spray from the nearby English Channel. The area had changed a great deal since 1869 and all that remained of the lavish grounds were the imposing holm oak, beech and cedar trees, which ran around the perimeter some fifty metres from the building. Their branches twisted and distorted by year upon year of unforgiving south westerly gales. The great storms of 1987 and 1990 had wreaked devastation as the south westerly winds of close to one hundred miles an hour slashed brutally through some of the more majestic oak trees uprooting them and leaving gaps that would never be replanted. Gone were the shrubs and bushes planted so carefully when the surrounding acres were laid out many years earlier. Sheep grazed near the perimeter fence and almost as a symbol of previous years of growth, clumps of their now discoloured wool torn from them as they brushed against the barbed wire fence still hung and waved erratically blown by every gust of wind.

Brian closed the car door and stood for a moment and took in the Gothic design mesmerised by the high and dark foreboding walls and symmetrical towers in front of him. The rooks rebuilding their nests in the trees nearest to the building squawked high above him distracted him momentarily before he turned to look out across the cliff tops and the dark rain clouds as they raced towards the coast. He shivered and pulled his overcoat collar up around his neck for protection and took a deep breath before he walked apprehensively towards the entrance and climbed the wide granite staircase.

He pressed the intercom and stated his name and a following a lengthy pause the electronic lock clicked open and the door was released. He walked into the waiting area and his attention was immediately drawn to a large garish multi-coloured poster.

Zing Zong
A musical and theatrical group of entertainers
will be here every Tuesday afternoon at 2:00 pm

As he moved from sign to sign he could hear the anguished screams that permeated the silence and echoed around the building. He subconsciously thrust his left hand into his overcoat and squeezed the keys harder and harder until they cut deep and painfully into his palm. Brian was oblivious to the pain as he continued to read the notices and rules stapled to every inch of cork boards. As he moved in front of a sensor the revolving door slowly rotated. He twisted his body and entered the reception area where the walls were covered with even more posters and cards.

A middle aged woman appeared at the reception window. Brian looked up and forced a smile. She pushed the toughened glass gently and it slid open a few inches. 'Can I help you?' she asked sternly.

Brian leaned towards the opening. 'I've come to visit, Sylvie . . . Sylvia Chapman,' he murmured softly and coughed nervously.

The receptionist tapped her keyboard, looked aimlessly into the air and waited. A few seconds later she nodded at the screen and gave him a furtive look.

'Relationship?'

'Pardon,' asked Brian.

'Your relationship with . . . er?' She checked the name on the screen. 'Er . . . Mrs Chapman?'

'Yes . . . Sylvia . . . she's my wife,' he replied.

'I need to know more than that,' she said firmly.

Brian looked at her and thought hard.

'I can tell you where we live?' he replied.

'Well, that's a start,' she said dismissively.

Brian gave her their address.

'How long have you lived there?' she asked.

Brian had to think.

'Twenty one years . . . a few months after we got married,' he said proudly.

She didn't acknowledge his reply and passed a card and pen through the open screen.

'Complete this and I'll see what I can do'. She closed the reception window and disappeared behind a row of towering wooden filing cabinets.

Brian carefully completed the form and waited. He suddenly became anxious and his fingers drummed on the wooden counter. He looked at his watch and then pressed the buzzer again.

The same woman appeared; slid open the window took the card and checked it. 'That's fine, Mr Chapman'. She smiled without looking directly at him. 'We can't be too careful . . . I'm sure you understand?'

Brian nodded with relief.

All signs of her smile suddenly disappeared as she continued. 'Before I let you in . . . er . . .' She looked at the form. '. . . Mr

Chapman, I must tell you that your wife is very ill'.

Brian took a step away from the window and lowered his head in shame.

'I know,' he murmured.

'Mr Chapman, your wife is heavily medicated and is in a world of her own . . . We need to do this for her own protection. In a few days . . .' She began to drawl as though she had said the same thing too many times before. 'If she responds positively we'll begin her treatment. But for now . . . Be patient . . . Be very patient . . .' She glared at him. 'And . . .' She paused, her expression changed and for the first time she stared directly at him. '*No* shocks!'

Brian stepped back apprehensively.

She continued. 'You will of course respect your wife and *all* our patients'. She screwed up her face. 'You see they all have very different issues . . . that's why they're in here'.

Brian tried to covey his understanding but failed.

His face remained blank.

She pressed a button, the lock was released and the inner door clicked open.

Brian entered the main vestibule. The exquisite floor to ceiling Devonshire marble pillars, supplied by Buckler of Dawlish, drew his eyes to the detailed cornices that had been retained with little damage except to accommodate the conduit for the emergency fire alarms and smoke detectors. The ornate oak doors had been removed many years earlier and replaced with plain fire doors part glazed with Georgian wired vision panels. The timber panelled walls had been painted in magnolia and the skirtings white which defaced what must once have been a beautiful building. An inner screen glazed with Georgian wired glass enclosed the whole area allowing visibility to the common area.

Brian thrust the flowers under his left arm and ran his right hand along the cast iron radiator that was now encrusted with layers of thick discoloured white gloss.

It felt warm and he welcomed it. He needed it.

The receptionist reappeared through a side door.

'Mr Chapman . . . we can only allow you to visit for half an hour'. She waited for Brian's response. There was none. 'I'm sure you understand?'

Brian nodded subserviently.

She looked down at the flowers Brian now held in his right hand. 'Oh . . . sorry, we don't allow flowers'.

Brian looked at her with utter contempt.

She feigned a smile before she spoke. 'You see some of our patients harm themselves and if they had a vase they might smash it . . .' She looked towards the ceiling. '. . . and then who knows what they'd do with the sharp pieces'. She paused and screwed up her face in disgust. 'Some even drink the water'.

Brian looked at her with utter disregard and reluctantly handed her the bouquet that he had so caringly chosen.

She pointed towards the long corridor. 'If you walk down there the nurse will be with you shortly,' she said. She pointed at the dark oak clock high on the wall. 'Don't forget . . . half an hour'. She held up the bouquet. 'Mr Chapman, you can collect these when you leave'.

She disappeared into her office and the door clicked behind her.

Brian stood in the corridor and while he waited he looked

intently at the framed pen and ink drawings of the grounds and surrounding area. The drawings that were undoubtedly commissioned when the lunatic asylum was built more than a hundred and forty years earlier were beginning to fade but nevertheless he found them intriguing. Oblivious to the pain he continued to squeeze the keys even deeper into his soft fleshy palm.

Nurses coaxed female patients as they shuffled blindly up and down the wide corridor with its painted oak panelled walls and encaustic floor tiles. Many of the patients talked to themselves while others held meaningless and agitated conversations with other patients.

Brian noticed a diminutive female Asian nurse who walked closely beside a hunched woman wearing an ankle length cotton nightshirt, white dressing gown and slippers. As the woman dragged her feet along the corridor the nurse continued to support her as her ill-fitting slippers flopped up and down as she walked on the worn tiles. Other patients moved zombie like, heads down, oblivious to anyone or anything around them.

The woman's hands shook erratically and her head twitched uncontrollably as she shuffled along the corridor. When Brian realised that it was Sylvia with the nurse he couldn't contain the shock and slumped heavily against the panelled wall and gasped for breath. He reached into his pocket, pulled out the inhaler now covered in deep red sticky blood and pushed it blindly between his lips and pumped it wildly.

The shock was unimaginable.

Sylvia's stylish dark hair had turned white within a few short days and it now hung lankly over her narrow hunched shoulders.

Brian wanted to hold her but remembered the receptionist's clear instructions and instead squeezed the keys once more. He could now feel the warm blood oozing between his fingers and into his pocket.

The nurse continued to support Sylvia as she shuffled down the corridor towards him. When the nurse saw him she nodded and turned into another corridor. Brian, still reeling at how Sylvia had deteriorated in such a short time, followed them at a distance, moving as slowly as he could without walking into them, through double doors, down another corridor and finally into what was the dining room for that wing.

Six tables, each with six chairs, odd salt and pepper pots in the centre of each table along with a plastic vase of faded fabric anemones. On one side were a few mismatched kitchen units, a dishwasher and fridge, and instead of a free standing kettle, which could scald anyone, a hot water boiler had been bolted to the wall. One wall was covered with stained, faded and ripped paintings and drawings created by long gone patients in their therapy and rehabilitation classes.

Many of the patients in the room wore identical patterned gowns and pink dressing gowns while some wore their own clothes. Brian assumed that the newer patients wore the matching gowns. A large West Indian lady, her thick black legs wide apart, smiled inanely at Brian as he entered. She mouthed unintelligible words to him and slobbered uncontrollably onto her clothes. Another woman cried intermittently and then screamed at the invisible person sitting at her table.

Brian smiled nervously at them but none of them were interested in the stranger.

The nurse sat Brian and Sylvia at a table next to the kitchen area.

It was clear Sylvia didn't know who Brian was and he looked to the nurse for answers.

There were none.

Brian could feel the despondency building up inside him and he wondered how long he could contain it.

The nurse sensed his despair and smiled at him before she turned her attention back to his wife. She leaned over Sylvia's shoulder and whispered in her ear. 'Syl . . . wie dis is . . . ?' She realised she didn't know the strangers name and looked at Brian for help.

Brian mouthed his name to her.

She thanked him with a submissive nod and a smile before she continued. 'Dis is Brian . . . he's come to visit with you,' she coaxed.

Sylvia didn't react.

The large lady on the other side of the room looked at him and formed an idiotic smile before she spoke. 'Bri . . . *Bri* . . . *Bri* . . . an . . . that's a nice name. Yeah . . .' She cackled loudly pleased with herself at being able to pronounce his name and continued to repeat Brian's name over and over until her voice faded away as she lost interest.

The nurse turned to Brian and pointed at a clock high on the wall.

'Hav en 'our . . . OK?' she said with a smile in her voice.

Brian nodded his agreement and the nurse left. He coughed nervously and cleared his throat. He was suddenly afraid to speak to his own wife.

He thought. *Was she his wife?*

He knew. *Of course she was.*

With his hands still in his pockets, he leaned on the edge of the table and for the first time looked directly at Sylvia.

Her grey dead eyes looked right through him and his whole body quivered uncontrollably as he began to appreciate her wretched condition and how ill she really was.

'Hello, Sylvia how are you?' He whispered.

She tilted her head to one side and replied. 'I'm fine,' she said softly. She sighed. 'Well . . . I am tired . . . but I'm having a rest'.

'How did you get in here?' asked Brian.

'I just arrived . . . All I wanted was to be safe . . . somewhere safe'. She thought hard before she continued. 'To get away from things'.

'What happened?' he probed.

'. . . fell down the stairs,' she said rapidly. She paused and shook her head erratically as she tried to remember. She suddenly remembered and continued excitedly. 'There was a bang and then I was falling down the stairs . . .' Her voice faded to a whisper as she expelled the remaining breath from her lungs.

Brian looked across at her; she was helpless and innocent.

She made to stand but then slumped back into the chair.

He wanted to hold her close to him but remembered that when he signed the form he had been told by the receptionist not to touch her. He didn't understand it at the time but now he knew the reason why.

Two elderly women cackled uncontrollably to each other and their high pitched voices reverberated around the room. Another woman sprang up from her table and began to scream the most obscene words at an empty chair, the pitch of her voice getting higher and higher as she became more and more agitated. Three nurses rushed into the room and dragged her away as she continued to scream.

Sylvia continued. 'I could see the street lights through the window,' she said excitedly. 'Looking for somewhere to live where my family can be safe from the world . . . a world that's'. She sighed heavily and blurted out. 'Changed!' Her face suddenly became racked with terror. She burst into tears and banged her hands on the table. 'Why? What are we all doing . . . ?' she screamed.

She looked around the room as though it was her first time. 'I arrived here'.

'Do you like it here?' asked Brian softly.

Her mood suddenly changed and she smiled inanely into space.

'I've got my own room'. She smiled childishly. 'I can have visitors . . . I get visitors . . .' she said excitedly. She looked around the room. '. . . sometimes'. She paused and tried to smile but her face twisted grotesquely. 'Do you like it here?'

'Well yes . . . as a matter of fact I do . . . I really do,' replied Brian feigning his enthusiasm.

'So do I'. Sylvia licked her lips. 'It's very nice . . . restful . . . quiet. Umm, it's nice,' she said softly.

Her eyes flitted across to the kitchen area.

'Fancy a coffee?' asked Brian.

'If it's all right,' she asked innocently.

'I'm sure it will be fine,' said Brian softly.

'Can I help you make it?' she asked.

Brian smiled genuinely for the first time. 'Of course you can,' he said.

Her face lit up, the childlike intensity unmistakeable as she held onto the table and pushed herself up. She shuffled towards the kitchen area and took a clean mug out of the dishwasher and placed it on the worktop several feet from him. 'You have this one . . .' She reached into the cupboard and took out a pink plastic beaker. 'I'll have this,' she said.

'Are you sure?' asked Brian.

'Course I am,' she replied curtly.

She pointed at the mug and for the first time Brian could see that her wrists were still heavily bandaged.

'I shouldn't use one of those,' she said shaking her head anxiously.

She checked the three casks looking for tea, coffee and sugar and opened the coffee. She tried to spoon the coffee into the mug and plastic cup but shook so much that she spilt it. Her frustration was clear as she slammed her hands on the worktop and screamed out. 'No . . . o . . . o . . . !'

Brian reached towards her; she stiffened and pulled away. Her fear stricken face twisted with horror.

He stepped away before speaking.

'It's all right . . . I can soon get that cleaned up,' he said reassuringly. He pointed to the table nearest the window. 'You sit down over there and I'll bring it over'. He smiled at her. 'In the plastic cup . . . Is that right?'

'Ye . . . eas,' she slurred and shook her head wildly.

Brian removed his bleeding hand from his pocket and washed away the congealed blood, dried it and wrapped several pieces of kitchen roll tightly around it before sliding it back into his pocket.

An elderly patient sidled up to him and he pulled back anxiously. She took a pale blue plastic cup from the dishwasher and filled it from the water heater and made a cup of tea. A split second later she pulled the tea bag from the cup and let it drip across the floor before dropping it into the open bin.

Brian wiped the floor and put the cloth back in the sink.

The woman then threw the tea down the sink and immediately made another cup and as she pulled the tea bag from the cup she dripped the tea across the floor in exactly the same place.

This time Brian ignored it and joined Sylvia at the table. He picked up the mug to drink his coffee but before he could taste it the Asian nurse stood at the door and beckoned him to leave.

He turned back to Sylvia. 'Shall I come and see you again?' he asked softly.

Sylvia nodded erratically and looked out of the window.

Brian emptied his cup in the sink and joined the nurse at the door. He looked across at Sylvia hoping for a reaction but she continued to stare out of the window.

He walked down the corridor in silence and as he walked through reception, the receptionist came out to him.

'Mr Chapman, could I have a word with you,' she asked sternly.

He stopped immediately and his face lacking all emotion stared directly at her.

'Please remember this is a hospital and our aim is to provide help and support for people who require a spell of care . . .' She looked hard a Brian and waited for his response. There was none. She coughed and continued. 'To help them cope with a wide range of conditions'. She paused. 'I'm sure you will help us to help them? Yes?'

Brian tilted his head and gave her a bewildered look.

The receptionist continued. 'Gresham House . . . is not a prison, detention centre or secure unit'. She smiled proudly. 'But we must be mindful of the reasons why people are here and protect them accordingly'.

Brian said nothing.

The receptionist handed him the flowers.

'I'm sure you understand?' she said.

Brian took them from her without uttering a word and signed out.

As he walked down the steps a mini bus pulled into the car park. Music blasted through the open windows. The whole van was spray painted with huge sun flowers and snakes that wound their way all over the van onto the roof and around the windows. The name 'Zing Zong' made up of intricate flowers and exotic fruit was painted down each side. A group of brightly dressed young students and hippies, their hands and arms tattooed and piercings in almost every conceivable place jumped out and grabbed an array of musical instruments and percussion from the rear of the vehicle. Their long matted hair and dreadlocks bounced around their shoulders as they raced each other up the wet steps, jumping two and three at a time.

Brian lowered his head and sobbed uncontrollably as he walked blindly across the car park his tears lost in the sudden heavy rain.

CHAPTER SIXTEEN

Make me an island

Brian pulled into the deserted company car park and locked his car. He stood and looked around at the vans that had been abandoned haphazardly by their drivers a few days earlier. He looked at his watch and remembered that none of the drivers worked for him any longer. He picked up the post, walked across to his desk, and opened it. He was interrupted by the ringing telephone. He looked at it and waited before he answered. 'Hello'.

'Good morning, this is Roger Saunders'.

Brian didn't speak.

'It's Roger Saunders from the Bank . . . Is that, Mr Chapman?'

'Speaking,' replied Brian.

'I've been asked to call you to tell you that Adams, Taylor & Partners have been appointed liquidators on behalf of the bank. They'll be with you as soon as they can.'

'Surprise, surprise,' replied Brian curtly. 'I guessed it would be them. Keeping it in the family, eh?'

Roger Saunders ignored him. 'I'd appreciate it if you and your wife could sign the forms for their appointment'.

'My wife is very ill in hospital so she won't be able to do that,' said Brian defiantly.

Roger Saunders paused for a minute. 'Well, I'm sure that won't be a problem if she's indisposed'.

Brian's response was met with silence.

Pam and Jackie arrived just as Brian slammed down the telephone.

'Sorry we're late, Brian,' said Jackie.

Brian looked at them. 'Late? You don't work for me any more'. He looked around the office. 'That's strange isn't it? I don't work here either'. He laughed with a high pitched screech. 'Crazy times eh?'

The both nodded.

'I know it's a silly question,' said Jackie, 'but is everything else alright?'

Brian shook his head vigorously.

'No . . .' he drawled.

They both looked at him aghast.

'Sylvie's poorly,' said Brian. 'Very poorly . . . she fell down the stairs'.

Pam and Jackie mouthed their shock. 'Fe—'

'Well . . . considering the calls we've been getting at home, I'm surprised she held out this long'.

They both looked surprised.

'She's been kept in for observation—'

'But she is alright?' asked Pam.

Brian nodded.

'She should be out in a day or two . . . you know how it is?'

Jackie saw the bouquet on the desk. 'Ooh . . . they're nice'.

'You can have 'em . . . Bloody hospital . . . Don't allow flowers these days'.

Pam looked on with envy as Jackie picked them and pecked Brian on the cheek.

Pam coughed.

'Brian . . . tell us about these calls,' she asked.

'Calls? Who were *they* from then?' asked Jackie.

'I'll give you three guesses . . .' He paused and smirked inanely. 'Four if you like,' he said.

'So what happened?' asked Pam.

'I went out for a takeaway and when I got back Sylvie was unconscious in the hall . . .' He remembered everything so vividly. His voice faded as he continued. 'She fell down the stairs'.

'What?' exclaimed Jackie.

'She's having tests just to be sure. You can't be too careful after falling down stairs. Internal injuries are very common apparently—'

'Pass on our love,' said Jackie as she thrust her nose deep into the flowers.

Brian nodded. 'Um . . .'

'Can we go in and see her?' asked Pam.

'No . . . No . . . No . . . Not at least for a few days,' replied Brian hastily. He paused briefly to think. 'They've got the Norwalk Virus in several of the wards . . . They're not allowing any visitors'.

Jackie and Pam looked at each other.

'Are you sure she's alright?' asked Jackie.

Brian faked a smile. 'Hospitals these days are filthy places you go in for a simple op . . . and you can come out worse than you went in . . . You know . . . MRSA and all that?'

Jackie looked directly at Brian and fluttered her eye-lashes.

'Well . . . you know where we are . . . Brian. If you do need anything . . . and I mean anything,' her voice tailed off.

Pam gave her a furtive look.

Brian smiled reassuringly.

'Thanks, but here's no need to worry,' he said.

'Really?' asked Jackie.

'Really, Sylvie will be fine,' he said.

'Well, you will let us know won't you? I expect she'll want a bit of female company?' said Jackie. 'No offence, Brian'. She licked her lips. 'Oh . . . and Brian if you need anything, washing, ironing, anything . . . just ask . . . The offer's there'.

Pam shot Jackie a look of total disbelief.

Brian nodded. 'Course . . . I'll tell you when . . .' His voice faded. 'Thanks for the offer'.

'We've been to the Job Centre,' said Pam.

'It's a crap place,' said Jackie.

They stood looking at him.

'Is there anything you want us to do now, Brian?' asked Jackie.

'I reckon we should sort out the purchase and sales ledgers, log books, the personnel files, holiday records and put it all together'. He looked at them. 'The bank has appointed Adams, Taylor & Partners'.

'Really? What about Fischer and Hager?' she asked.

'David told me it's the bank's final decision'. Brian frowned. 'Well, I'm going to the infamous Job Centre; I should be about an hour'. He turned. 'Oh, and when our visitors come make them uncomfortable for me'.

*

Brian parked his car in the car park at the rear of the Job Centre and walked in. It was the first time in his working life that he had ever needed to go there.

A man in a cheap and ill-fitting suit stood at the top of the stairs. 'Can I help you, sir?' asked the young man reaching for his clip board.

'I've come to register,' said Brian.

'Initials?' he asked brusquely.

'Brian Chapman,' replied Brian.

'Ah . . . BC,' said the man. He pointed towards a row of desks. 'You need "C," over there. Take a seat and they'll call you'.

He turned his attention to the young girl immediately behind Brian. 'Can I help, miss?' he asked patronisingly.

Brian walked across to the waiting area and took a seat beneath a sign with the letters 'A-D.'

Twenty minutes later he heard his name being called out over the tannoy.

'Mr Chapman . . . could you come to desk one'.

Brian looked towards the desk and saw a spotty teenager looking around expectantly.

Brian walked across to the desk and sat down.

'Can I help you, sir?' asked the young man.

'I hope so. I've come to register?'

'Name?' asked the clerk abruptly.

Brian looked around before speaking. 'Brian Chapman'.

'Oh!' exclaimed the clerk. 'Brian Chapman? Ah, you shouldn't be *here* they've opened a special office for your company'. He pointed across the office to a door marked *Private*. 'You need to wait in there . . . Most of your lot have already signed and gone—'

Brian stormed off in disgust and entered the room.

Eric, Steve, Conrad, Colin Corke, Craig and Natasha were the last of his employees waiting for their interview.

Craig glared at Brian, mumbled under his breath and stormed out of the room dragging Natasha with him.

Brian glared back at him as he passed, took a deep breath and resisted the urge to lash out. Instead he walked across to the others.

'Hello, Eric, Conrad, morning, Colin . . . Steve,' said Brian.

Steve turned away from him and cursed under his breath.

'I didn't expect to back here so soon,' said Colin.

'I didn't ever expect to be here,' said Brian.

Eric looked at both of them and smiled innocently.

Brian and Jackie stood in his office sifting through various files. Brian's mobile rang.

'Hi, Brian, it's Steven Slade'.

'Oh . . . hello, Steven, how are you?' asked Brian in a pained voice.

'I'm fine thanks, Brian. I hear you've had a bit of bad luck, do you want to come in and talk about it on air . . . tell our listeners about it . . . pre-empt the gossip and lies?'

Brian didn't reply.

Steven continued. 'Brian, it would be an ideal opportunity for you to tell our listeners the truth rather than wait until they read lies in the papers'.

Brian took a deep breath before he replied. 'Yeah, of course I will. Let me give you a call tomorrow and we'll fix a date and time. Thanks, Steven'.

As he slipped his mobile into his pocket the office door burst open and in rushed three heavily built men wearing dirty white tee-shirts and jeans. Every inch of visible skin was heavily tattooed. Two of them had long pony tails, earrings and nose studs.

Brian and Jackie stood routed to the spot.

'We've come for the vans,' demanded the largest of the three.

Brian looked at him for a moment before speaking. 'I beg your pardon,' he said politely.

The man thrust a piece of paper into Brian's hand.

Brian looked at it and as he acknowledged defeat passed it to Jackie.

Her whole body shook as she took her time to read it. Her hand dropped to her side as she looked across to Brian.

He nodded his reply and mumbled. 'Yeah . . .'

She reread it and carefully checked the registration numbers listed on the paper.

'Yes, they're ours . . .' She looked across at Brian and then the three men before taking a huge breath. She straightened her body and looked at them defiantly. 'What do you mean . . . you've come to collect them?' she asked.

'You've gone bust.' He laughed loudly. 'You're fucked!'

'We want 'em . . . now!' screamed the second man.

'Get the keys!' yelled the biggest of the three and clearly their leader.

Brian picked the phone on his desk and trembled as he dialled David's number and waited.

'Good morning David, I've got three men here . . .' he gasped. 'They say they've come for our vans'.

'That's right Brian. They're "repo" men . . . Your vans are being re-possessed'.

Brian replaced the telephone, walked across the office took the keys from the metal box on the wall and handed them over.

The three men looked at each other and grinned with satisfaction.

'There you are,' said the leader. 'It wasn't so bad was it?' He laughed loudly. He checked his paperwork. 'What about these two?' he pointed at the registration numbers on the sheet.

'They were stolen by the men,' replied Brian.

One of the repo men laughed loudly. 'Did they now?' he snarled and turned to the others. 'I like it when they do that . . . we'll break their legs if they—'

The leader reached out, grabbed his arm and squeezed it firmly. The man recoiled in excruciating pain.

The second man snatched all the keys from Brian, scribbled his signature on the paper and threw it onto the floor.

They stormed out of the office slamming the door behind them.

Brian sat at the end of his desk and tried to catch his breath.

A very shocked Jackie looked at him. 'Coffee?'

Brian nodded.

Jackie returned almost immediately and tried to hide her embarrassment. 'We haven't got any milk . . .' she said. 'Is black alright?'

Brian ignored her and unable to hide his despair slumped into the nearest chair and thrust his head into his shaking hands.

Jackie passed Pam at the door and stood in front of them trembling. 'You'd better come with me, Brian.' She turned her head towards him. 'But you won't like it'.

The three of them stood in the workshop. Boxes had been broken open, glasses smashed, hand tools were strewn all over the floor and the security cages, which usually held power tools, the expensive electrical and heating parts, had been ripped open leaving only empty boxes.

They all stood and tried to take in the destruction.

'Brian, we've been robbed,' stuttered Jackie.

Brian picked up a damaged router; it had been left to go back for repair but Craig hadn't got around to it.

'I don't think so, Jackie,' said Brian. 'The door hasn't been forced'. He walked over and tried it. 'It's still locked. No, whoever did this,' He shook his head and took a deep breath. 'And I can think of quite few who had keys . . . stole it!'

He slumped to his knees.

Jackie looked at him and then Pam. 'I'm going to call the police,' she said.

Half an hour later a police car swept into the car park, blue lights flashing and siren wailing. The two policemen rushed towards the building and into the workshop where they joined Brian, Pam and Jackie. They took a few moments to survey the damage before either of them spoke.

'Tell me, Mr Chapman,' asked the police sergeant. He paused as he opened his notebook. 'You've recently closed the business?'

The second policeman interrupted and gave a wide smile. 'I saw you on TV, last night on the local news . . . terrible eh?'

Jackie glared at him.

The police sergeant coughed and the second policeman straightened up.

'You have reason to believe that this damage was caused by one or several of your employees?'

'Ex-employees, sergeant,' said Jackie.

He coughed again. 'Yes, of course . . . Your ex-employees,'

he repeated as he looked around the workshop. 'You say there are a lot of items missing?'

Brian nodded. 'That's right,' said Brian as he looked around at the destruction. 'It will take a while but we should be able to give you a list of most of it from our stock, tool and plant lists'.

The two policemen looked at each other and frowned.

'I see,' said the police sergeant. 'Do you have any idea who might be responsible for this?'

Brian looked at Pam and then Jackie.

They all nodded.

'Yes, we have,' said Brian.

The police sergeant looked at Jackie and Pam before he finally turned to Brian. 'We're faced with a very difficult situation here, Mr Chapman'. He flicked through his note book. 'As you are no longer in business . . . it is unlikely that we're going to recover any of these items'.

They all looked at him in sheer disbelief.

'And, as for us interviewing them . . .' He paused. 'How many employees did you say you had?' asked the second policeman.

'Over fifty,' said Pam.

Jackie interrupted her. 'Fifty three . . . no . . . fifty four to be precise. We took on a new engineer, Colin Corke, a few weeks before we . . .' She stopped mid-sentence and blushed.

'Um . . .' He thought. 'We'd need to interview everyone and whilst you may have your suspicions as to who did this we obviously can't only pay those a visit—'

'Why not?' screamed Brian.

He shook his head and kicked out angrily at the empty boxes.

'We need to interview everyone,' said the policeman.

He looked up from his notebook and continued. 'Including yourselves'.

There were gasps of disbelief.

'Us?' they all said.

Jackie shook her head. 'Interview me?' She paused. 'So you think I stole tools . . . parts. Me . . . ?'

The police sergeant looked directly at her. 'Yes, we need to interview everyone to establish proof. There may be others in collusion and witnesses to the alleged theft. If we are to have any likelihood of a conviction we need proof and or course witnesses'.

'Did you see anyone steal these items, Mr Chapman?' he asked.

Brian shook his head.

The police sergeant looked directly at him.

'Well, Mr Chapman, do you know how many companies are in a similar situation to yourself? Employees are owed money, wages, holiday pay and whatever . . .' He shook his head and tried to imagine. 'They see this as a way of getting what's due to them'.

'But its criminal!' raged Brian.

'Of course it is,' said the second policeman, 'but it's going to take a lot of police time. We'll report it to the C.I.D . . . but . . .' He paused and looked around at the wanton damage. 'What are we looking at here?' he shrugged his shoulders. 'Four . . . maybe five thousand pounds?'

Brian nodded in agreement.

'Plus the vans they took,' said Jackie.

The police sergeant nodded.

'They're easy to find . . . With respect, that's the least of your problems'.

'I'm sure the liquidators will get onto the culprits . . . they have a way of getting vehicles back,' he said with a smile.

'Yeah, we met them earlier,' said Jackie, shuddering as she remembered the repo men.

The policeman looked at Brian nervously and cleared his throat. 'I doubt if they'll want to follow this lot up . . . it will take up a considerable amount of police resources and if we do recover some of it the liquidators will only sell it at knock down prices . . .'

'And you won't see the benefit of it . . . Mr Chapman,' said the police sergeant.

Brian shrugged. 'Just like that,' he cursed. 'So we're all wasting our time . . . is that right?'

The police sergeant was clearly embarrassed and he coughed before he replied. 'We'll let you have a crime number for your . . .' He paused and coughed nervously before he continued. 'For your insurance company . . . in case the liquidators do want to follow it up but apart from that, there's little else we can do'.

'Can't you go and see the culprits if we give you their addresses?' screamed Brian.

'They'll probably have the vans outside their homes,' said Jackie.

'No . . . it's all or nothing,' said the police sergeant. 'Sorry, Mr Chapman'.

'The liquidators will get those,' said the policeman. 'You wait and see'.

The police sergeant tore a page from his note book and handed Brian a crime number. They closed their note books and slipped them into their pockets.

'Good to meet you, Mr Chapman, ladies'.

The policemen cast a furtive look around, turned and walked out.

Brian, Pam and Jackie stood and looked on in silence.

'Anything you fancy here, ladies?' said Brian angrily. 'Help yourselves, everybody else has!'

Brian stormed out.

CHAPTER SEVENTEEN

How deep is your love

Brian drove to his mother's house and let himself in. She was in the kitchen washing the lunchtime dishes; a plate, cup and saucer, knife and spoon. She heard Brian behind her and turned. 'Well? How is she?'

'She's very poorly, mum . . .'

She gave him a look of concern.

'Well what do you expect?' He sighed. 'She fell down the whole flight of stairs and cut herself as well as whatever else she's done internally'.

'What ward is she in? I must go in and see her—'

'No!' snapped Brian.

'What? Of course I must'. She thought. 'And so must you . . .'

'Norwalk . . . they've got Norwalk in the hospital and won't allow visitors . . . at least not for the minute'.

'Can I telephone her?' she asked.

'No . . . no . . . not at the moment . . . she's far from well,' he lied.

'Well you make sure you leave a message for her . . . a hospital is a very lonely place. I remember when I was in there after my knee operation. It was no better than prison . . . and the food . . . How are they allowed to dish up such?' She paused and rubbed her knee. 'Well, you know what I mean'.

Brian nodded.

He'd lied to his own mother.

Brian waited in the corridor and watched as the nurses helped their patients up and down the corridor. The Asian nurse arrived and acknowledged him before leading him towards the canteen.

'How is she?' whispered Brian.

The nurse gave him a positive nod.

Sylvia sat at a table and faced the wall.

Brian stood a few feet behind her and listened to her rambling.

'Yes, a house. I don't want anything flash . . . a small house . . . nothing too . . .' She paused. 'Nothing flash,' she said. She stood up and then immediately sat down again. 'What am I doing here? I only need something small . . . Somewhere to get away from . . . ? Here . . . It'll cost a fortune . . . all I want is a house . . . nothing flash'. She lapsed into a stupor and it was several minutes before she was able to continue. 'I turned around and the lady was there again. We've found you a house,' she said. 'I remember smiling . . . A house . . . for me and my family? I felt so excited and happy . . . I've got a house'. She tried to remember. 'We walked into a room . . . No!' She began to shake uncontrollably. 'I asked for a basic house! But this is one room . . . Not even a wash hand basin . . . No! I want a house . . . not a flat!'

Brian looked visibly concerned.

He sat down at the next table and waited for her to stop talking.

'I'm sure you'll get your house . . .' he said softly. He paused and took a few deep breaths before he continued. 'But you need to get better first'.

She stared at him while she thought about what he'd said.

'I remember this huge black woman giving me a capsule and a drink of water'.

She looked slowly around the room.

'And here I am . . .' She shook her head and lowered her voice to a whisper. 'You know . . . all I wanted was a house and now . . . I'm here'.

Brian wiped his eyes, turned and made his way towards the closed door.

As he opened the door Sylvia spoke.

'How's Jenny?' she said timidly.

Brian froze with shock. He turned and took a step towards her as the widest smile appeared across his once sad face.

'She's fine and so's Jamie,' he said softly.

The feeling of sheer joy he experienced that moment was unimaginable. He swallowed hard.

'What about Sammy?' she asked.

'We're all fine. You take your time and get better . . . that's what we all want,' he said softly.

He smiled at her and nodded slowly.

'Bye, Sylvie . . . See you next time'.

She lifted her arm and gave a gentle wave.

Brian shed tears of sheer elation as he walked down the corridor.

She had remembered everyone including Sammy but not him; her husband.

He stood at the top of the steps and looked through the trees and out to sea and at that moment the sun burst through the thick cloud and the warm rays touched his face. For the first time in many days he felt encouraged.

The sun began to dry the rain soaked walls and briefly even the hand cut limestone looked warm.

By the time Brian arrived back at his car he had six messages on his mobile, mostly requests for more radio and television interviews and journalists from local and regional newspapers. He listened to each of them before turning his phone off. When he arrived at his office he couldn't believe what he saw. The car park was crammed with BMW's and other executive cars. Brian walked into the general office and was confronted by a mass of strangers. The only people he recognised apart from Pam and Jackie was Allan Taylor of Adams, Taylor and Partners.

'Hello, Brian. This is my team,' said Allan Taylor.

Brian fired him a hard look.

'What's going on?' he asked.

Allan Taylor ignored his question and pointed at a young man in a dark suit leaning across Pam's desk. 'This is, John Fitzgerald'.

Before Brian had time to comment he pointed at another young woman wearing the obligatory dark suit. 'This is, Rachel Hinds'.

They each acknowledged Brian with a phoney and no doubt well-rehearsed smile.

'We have frozen the company bank account and Rachel will visit you every few days and collect any cheques you receive and we will bank them in the new account.'

154

Rachel spoke for the first time. 'I need every cheque you receive and I would suggest two of you open all the post,' she said firmly. 'And we will need sight of your up to date sales ledger so we can chase the outstanding debtors.'

Brian looked at her and then back to Allan Taylor. 'What?' he asked.

Allan Taylor responded. 'As part of our appointment we have opened a client account and will place any receipts into it until such time as we feel we can complete our work and formally dissolve the company.'

Another stranger entered the office and interrupted the liquidator. 'Allan, can I have the log books now?'

Allan Taylor walked across the office and stood next to yet another man in a dark suit. 'Just a minute, Brian'. He waited until he had Brian's attention. 'Brian, this is Barry Knight, the auctioneer'.

'Auctioneer! What do you mean auctioneer?' questioned Brian clearly in a state of shock.

Allan Taylor stood erect and spoke with authority. 'Mr Chapman, as Liquidators we have to realise as many of the assets as quickly as possible. The bank has a fixed and floating charge over the contents and building. Remember? You signed it'. He held up a copy of the letter Brian and Sylvia had signed a few short weeks earlier. 'These are your signatures?'

Brian nodded.

'I doubt of they will be much left after that,' said Fitzgerald.

Allan Taylor looked at Brian and sensing his anger guided him towards the door. 'Come on, Brian let's go to your office'. He turned to Pam. 'Coffee . . . two sugars'.

*

155

Brian stood behind his desk and looked around at his hard work. Remembering how it had all been put together and the lengthy deliberation in deciding on the colour scheme and carefully choosing the photographs and frames.

Allan gave Brian a stern look before sitting on one of the settees. 'You know you shouldn't have dismissed your staff.'

Brian walked towards him. 'What do you mean? We had *no* money to pay them let alone our suppliers.' He paused. 'In fact I couldn't pay anyone . . . . So how do you work that out?'

'Listen, Brian. We would normally administer the business. Keep it trading and look to find a buyer—'

'Buy what!' screamed Brian.

'Well . . . we could have tried to sell the business as a going concern . . . but as you got rid of *everyone* we have nothing to sell.' Allan Taylor stood and looked directly at Brian. 'I know this is not easy Brian but I want you to identify anything that is yours.' He lowered his voice and continued. 'We will of course require proof'.

Brian's face drained of all colour.

'Tell me . . . Allan'. He sucked through his teeth. 'How is it that people can just walk in and steal someone else's property and get away with it?' he asked cynically.

Before Allan Taylor could answer Brian's question the auctioneer walked in with a clipboard and a handful of labels.

'Is there anything of Mr Chapman's in here?' he asked.

Allan looked at Brian and waited for an answer.

'Could I have a few minutes?' muttered Brian.

The auctioneer tapped his clipboard impatiently. 'I need to get this wrapped up in the next hour'. He smiled. 'I've got two more this afternoon'.

As the auctioneer walked through the doorway he was

pushed aside by a middle aged man followed closely by a stressed Jackie.

'I don't give a damn what he's meeting or who he's meeting! I want my money!' screamed the man.

Allan Taylor had his back to the door and slowly turned around.

The man stood shaking and waving his fist at Brian. 'Come on, you bastard! You owe me five hundred and fifty three quid! Where is it? I want it now!'

Brian was taken by total surprise and didn't know how to deal with it.

'Mr Greaves?' he asked.

'Yeah, you know who I am alright . . . Where's my money?'

'This is Mr Taylor, the liquidator,' said Brian pointing nervously at Allan.

'Liquidator? Fucking leeches, if you ask me.' He turned to Brian. 'I want my M . . . O . . . N . . . E . . . Y . . . Now!'

Brian stared at him and tried to get the words out. 'B . . . b . . . but I haven't g . . . g . . . got it, Mr Greaves'.

'All right,' he said arrogantly. 'Give me the keys to one of the vans . . . I don't care which one'.

'I can't do that,' said Brian looking across at the liquidator.

'You certainly can't. I'm in control of this company now!' said Allan Taylor.

The man looked directly at the liquidator. 'You give me the keys then'.

'Now listen to me, Mr Greaves?'

'Yeah?' he replied sharply.

Allan Taylor walked towards him.

'Listen to me carefully, Mr Greaves'.

Mr Greaves straightened and waited.

Allan Taylor continued. 'Nothing must leave these offices, or the car park. Our plans are to auction everything and if you want to bid for anything . . . anything at all . . . then of course you may'.

Mr Greaves kicked out the settee.

'This is the fifth company to do this to me this year and I've not got a fucking penny from any of them'. He punched the air. 'Come on give me the fucking keys . . . the oldest van will do . . .' He looked at each of them in turn and waited.

There was only silence.

He continued. 'I'm not fussy,' he snarled.

Allan Taylor turned to Brian. 'Mr Chapman, I must formally advise you that you cannot, I repeat cannot, hand over any of the assets of this company'.

Mr Greaves turned, kicked out at the other settee and gave both of them an intimidating glower. 'I'll get my money . . . you bastards! Fucking leeches!' He turned and stormed out of the office slamming the door. The keys dropped out of the lock and onto the carpet.

Allan Taylor showed genuine concern for the first time. 'He's a nasty piece of work'.

Brian nodded before he gathered his thoughts and spoke. 'He's been good to us but I do understand his situation.' He took a deep breath and sighed heavily. 'Like me he's struggling to survive.' He reflected. 'Well, I was . . .'

Allan Taylor looked towards the door and waited until he heard Mr Greaves stomp down the stairs and the front door slam. 'I must warn you, Brian . . . there will be others'.

Brian slumped into his chair but when he heard the auctioneer clomping up the stairs he jumped out of his chair and removed the photographs from the wall and pictures from his desk.

He dropped one of the company photographs behind a filing cabinet and couldn't reach it before the auctioneer bounced into the office. Brian picked up his laptop, printer, hard drive and selected items from his desk and slipped them into his case.

Craig Jameson and Natasha lay on the settee in her flat and watched television. When Brian appeared on the screen they both sat up.

'Look at that smug bastard,' said Craig.

'Yeah, look at him, he's on again . . . what a bastard and I'll tell him to his face. He's got no idea, no fucking idea,' said Natasha.

'He's certainly wrecked things for us,' he seethed.

Brian sat at his desk and worked his way through a mound of files before shredding them in a machine beside him.

Jackie rushed into his office and stopped a few inches from his desk. 'Brian, you should see this!'

She passed him the letter and Brian read it twice before he spoke.

'How the hell can they say that? I'll get lynched!' He reached for the telephone and dialled the liquidator. 'Allan, what the hell is this about?' He shook his head wildly. 'You told me that everyone would get redundancy and outstanding holiday pay. This letter says the opposite . . . No! It clearly states that employees will receive nothing . . .' He hammered on his desk. 'Allan, let me tell you this . . . if you don't retract that and send out a new letter to everyone . . . I mean everyone . . . confirming what you told me the day you took over the business . . . then there is no way . . .' He gasped. 'I mean no fucking way that I'm going to sit there on Thursday and be castigated and insulted by those bastards . . .' He punched at his desk. 'Do me a favour and get them out today and email me a copy . . . because I'm telling you now it could get very nasty . . . very nasty indeed!'

He threw down the phone and kicked out at his desk.

Brian and David parked near the entrance of the hotel booked for the creditors meeting and immediately their car was surrounded by Craig, Natasha, Conrad and a group of his distraught employees. Colin Corke hung back.

David guided Brian through the sneering group and into the hotel room booked for the meeting.

The room was laid out theatre style with a raised platform at one end with a table and seven chairs. Allan, John Fitzgerald and Rachel Hinds were grouped around a table adjacent to the platform drinking coffee. While they acknowledged Brian and David a young waitress poured them all coffee.

Brian walked across to Allan. 'Hello, Allan did you get the letters out?'

Allan lowered his cup and saucer and appeared sheepish. 'We did . . .'

Brian looked at him suspiciously. 'Are you sure you did . . . ?' He gasped for air and spluttered.

Allan nodded.

'When?' asked Brian.

Allan murmured. 'Yesterday . . .'

'What the fuck!' screamed Brian. 'What did I tell you? That's all those bastards out there needed . . . an excuse . . . and you gave it to 'em on a plate!'

He turned to David the fury exploding across his anger stricken face.

David lowered his outstretched fingers and murmured to him. 'Ssh . . . don't worry, Brian . . . you're not on your own'.

Brian screamed out. 'Not here but I will be after this fucking circus finishes . . . !'

He turned and kicked out at the rows of chairs. They clattered off the platform.

Allan Taylor unaffected by Brian's outburst checked his watch and moved towards the stand while the waitress rushed around and picked up the chairs and rearranged them in neat rows. 'Ladies, gentlemen, can we all take out seats please?' he said.

They took their seats and left the three central chairs for Brian, David and the absent Sylvia.

The waitress opened the side door and left the room.

The first people to enter were three men in dark suits each carrying a briefcase. They sat in the front row and opened their files. They were followed by all the engineers and Natasha who kept close to Craig. The two of them sat a few rows back with Conrad and their remaining workmates clustered around them. Colin Corke, Pam, Jackie and Eric sat in the back row and watched nervously.

Allan stood up and addressed the attendees. 'Good afternoon ladies and gentlemen. My name is Allan Taylor and I am the appointed liquidator of Brian Chapman Services Limited'. He paused to look at his notes and began to read. 'Brian Chapman Services Limited was incorporated on 4 August 1995 and had two directors and shareholders, namely, Sylvia Julie Chapman and Brian George Chapman of 43 Barley Lodge Road Milton'.

Craig and Natasha smirked at Brian.

Allan Taylor stared at them and waited until they blushed with embarrassment and lowered their heads. He looked along the table at Brian and the empty chair and continued. 'Unfortunately, Sylvia Chapman could not be here today due to ill health'. He coughed and continued. 'But I can tell you that having carried out an exhaustive audit of the business we could find no impropriety'.

The engineers mumbled incoherent noises in response.

Allan Taylor shot them a stern look and continued. 'The reason we are here today is for one reason only . . . simply a lack of positive cash flow'. He looked directly at Craig. 'Something that is synonymous with the current recession'. He turned the page. 'There was a shortfall of four hundred thousand pounds which is attributable to HM Inspector of Revenue and Customs, the Alford Bank, Devon County Council and Gerrard Builders Merchants plus utility companies, British Gas, Western Power and South West Water'.

As the creditor's names were read out the suited men scribbled eagerly.

Allan Taylor continued. 'Before I declare the meeting of creditors closed are there any questions?'

Craig was the first to shout out. 'When am I getting my fucking wages?'

He stabbed his finger forcefully in Brian's direction.

Brian moved nervously in his chair and clawed at his suit jacket beneath the table.

'That bastard owes me two weeks pay and me holiday money!' screamed Craig, his face grew red with the intense anger; he made a fist and shook it angrily at Brian. 'I've got a wife and kids!'

The rest of the group stood up and jeered and shouted at Brian. 'Yeah . . . What about us!'

Brian was about to speak but David grabbed at his arm.

Natasha stood up and with the contempt cutting through her young voice she screamed at Brian. 'Why did that thick bastard spend money on a poxy video . . . if he knew he didn't have the money?'

They all jeered and punched the air. 'Yeah'.

Brian replied but his voice was drowned out by the jeers. 'She's a fucking trainee for God sake . . . she's got no right!'

David tried to quell Brian's anger. He stood up and pushed his chair to one side. 'I've known Brian and Sylvia for more than twenty years and I know they have sacrificed a great deal to keep their business trading . . . and . . . you!' He couldn't contain his anger any longer and pointed directly at Craig and Natasha. 'To keep you all in jobs!'

They continued to jeer and heckle him.

Allan Taylor rose from his chair and stood erect cutting a formidable character. Without looking down he reached out, picked up the water jug and brought it down heavily onto the table. 'I want order . . . NOW!'

For the first time there was total silence and he continued in a controlled voice. 'Official creditors will be advised in due course of any payments we are likely to be able to make'. He glared at Craig and Natasha. 'I declare this meeting closed . . . thank you for coming'.

Allan shook Brian's hand and mouthed to him. 'Sorry . . .'

Brian pulled his hand away and flanked by David walked out of the hotel.

They walked towards David's car but before he could unlock it Craig and several of the others raced towards them and lashed out at Brian knocking him to the ground. David forced his way between them and hurriedly grabbed Brian and bundled him into the car.

CHAPTER EIGHTEEN

Help me make it through the night

Brian stretched out on the settee, with a large brandy and reflected on the day's events while Sammy nuzzled into him. Sammy suddenly let out a deep throaty growl and then Brian heard the footsteps on the gravel path. A scaffold pole crashed through the window and stopped several metres inside the lounge and a metre from Brian's feet. Sammy raced around the room in a frenzy, barked uncontrollably, jumped at the curtains and growled at the improvised missile.

Jamie rushed into the lounge.

'Dad, what the hell was that?' he screamed.

Brian tried desperately to calm Sammy down. 'Don't worry, just a bit of a problem. I can't understand these people,' he said shaking his head. 'Don't they know when enough is enough—?'

'Who would do that?' screamed Jamie.

Brian looked at him through his sad tired eyes.

'I don't know for sure, son but it's probably one of the bastards from the company'.

Brian grabbed at the scaffold pole, pulled it into the lounge and laid it on the carpet.

Jamie looked down at him. 'What! One of the men who used to work for . . . ?'

'I'm afraid so,' replied his father despondently.

The phone rang and Jamie picked it up. 'Yes, who is it?' Jamie covered the mouth piece. 'It's somebody swearing, dad'.

'Put it down, Jamie. Just put it down!' he screamed

Jamie replaced the phone and shook uncontrollably before breaking into tears. 'How could they change like that?' He sobbed. 'I mean you looked after them all. What changed?'

'The recession changed everything, Jamie . . . including people'. He paused and reached out to his son. 'Jamie?'

'Yes dad?'

'Not a word to your Nan about this'. He pointed his index finger menacingly at his son and waited. 'All right?'

A shocked Jamie looked back at his father and trembled as he spoke. 'Yes, dad'.

Jamie held the cannibalised dining table, its legs sawn off, against the window while Brian reluctantly drilled through the face as a makeshift means of securing the opening.

Brian held back his tears as he tightened the last of the screws, pulled the curtains and left the room.

'Come on, Jamie . . . bed'.

Jamie turned out the light and followed his father upstairs.

By the time Brian left Gresham House it was getting dark. He made his was along the dual carriageway in silence; his mind elsewhere. Unable to take any more of the continual depressing news he turned off the radio and slid the Zing Zong CD he'd bought from the group into the player. As the first song played he felt good, the best he'd felt for several weeks. He stopped at the traffic lights and saw Colin Corke's brand new company van pull up beside him. He looked across, saw Natasha in the passenger seat and then noticed Craig was driving.

Natasha nudged Craig and when he saw Brian he smirked at him and gave him the finger as he gunned the accelerator.

The lights were still red.

As soon as the light flashed amber Brian pulled away while Craig revved the engine before he accelerated so hard that his tyres smoked as he roared away.

Brian felt a bump and looked around.

Craig and Natasha pulled level with Brian and both of them gave him the 'V' sign.

Brian ignored them and continued to drive.

Craig drove close to Brian's offside and turned his wheel hard into the side of Brian's car in an attempt to force Brian off the road.

Brian grabbed hard at the steering wheel and struggled to maintain control as Craig crashed into him again and again forcing Brian into the Armco, the metal crash barrier. Sparks flew in every direction as the nearside wing was ripped off, the doors were crushed and windows smashed.

Natasha continued to scream obscenities at Brian through the open window as Craig smashed into the side of Brian's Audi for the fifth time.

Brian struggled to maintain control of his car and seeing a garage up ahead steadied the car sufficiently to reach it. He drove onto the forecourt, turned sharp left and drove directly at the cashier's window, braking at the very last minute. Craig realising what Brian had done gave yet another 'V' sign before accelerating away along the dual carriageway in an equally battered vehicle.

Brian had just seen his glittering business past and future

destroyed in a split second. He slumped forward exhausted and shaken.

'Are you alright, sir,' asked the Sikh cashier through the forecourt intercom.

Brian forced open the driver's door and staggered out.

'I . . . I . . . think so,' he murmured.

'I saw what happened. If you want me to give the police a witness statement . . .' gushed the cashier, 'and we've probably got some of it on CCTV'.

'Thanks for your offer but I think we'd be wasting our time,' said Brian. 'But thanks all the same'. He surveyed the extensive damage to his car and found he was unable to open the fuel cap. He slipped the catch and took a petrol can from the open boot; the only part of his vehicle not damaged, and filled it. He walked across to the pay desk and passed his credit card through the open window.

The cashier loaded it into the machine and waited. The machine bleeped at him and he tried again before he removed the card and handed it back to Brian. 'Sorry, sir . . . it's been refused'.

Without saying a word Brian returned to his car and systematically searched every compartment, beneath the floor mats, the ashtray and pockets until he'd collected every coin he could find. He returned to the pay desk and slid the handful of coins through the window. The cashier counted and recounted the money. He flicked the microphone and his voice crackled through the speakers filling the silence of the forecourt. 'You're 45p short, sir,' he said.

Brian slumped to his knees and screamed out.

The cashier's distorted voice shrieked over the tannoy. 'Don't worry, sir it looks like you need a bit of help'. The microphone began to feedback and a high pitched whistle filled the air until the cashier fiddled with the switch and turned it off. He then counted some of the unclaimed loose change in the tray in front of him and slipped it into the till. The distorted voice boomed out once more. 'I've got that, sir' he said.

Brian grunted his reply, pushed himself to his feet and shuffled towards his car.

The Sikh cashier looked out across the forecourt and found it hard to hide his feelings as he empathised with the difficulties his customer was going through. He bent his head, spoke into the microphone and his tense voice crackled across the forecourt tannoy. 'Are you *sure* you don't want me to call the police, sir?' He paused. 'Why don't you come back and I'll call them. I'm sure they will be able to help you, sir'.

Brian shook his head awkwardly as he continued to walk slowly away. He reached his car and blind to the damage he tugged at the crushed door. As he started the engine his hands free mobile rang.

'Hi Brian . . . you're a hard man to get hold of these days,' said the voice at the other end.

Brian looked into space and grunted his agreement. 'Um . . .'

'Is that you Brian? It's Richard Parker'.

Brian didn't answer him.

'Brian, it's Richard Parker, I shot the video for you?'

Brian growled his response.

'Listen, Brian, I need you to pay me for it now! The bank is chasing me . . . I've got the crew to pay . . . plus the editor and the music—'

Brian flicked at the phone and ripped the microphone out of the visor.

CHAPTER NINETEEN

Sounds of silence

Brian drove up the drive, switched off the engine and again as he forced the car door open it scraped noisily against the distorted and twisted bodywork. He could hear Sammy barking and when he opened the front door Sammy jumped up at him. 'What's a matter, boy?'

Sammy continued to bark as he chased around wildly.

'Alright, calm down, Sammy. What on earth is wrong?'

Brian opened the lounge door and flicked the light switch.

It didn't work.

He scrabbled around on the floor until he found a table light. He turned it on and took a step back. He tripped and when he picked himself up he looked around in disbelief. The plasma television screen was smashed; video and DVD players lay smashed in the centre of the room, the furniture covered in black gloss paint and sprayed in red letters on the wall were the words — *Bastard! Cheat!*

The room was wrecked.

Brian tried to console Sammy while he took in what had happened to his house.

He felt defiled.

He tried his mobile but it had no life left in it. The battery was totally flat. He up righted the settee and ignoring the wet gloss paint splashed all over it, he sat down and cried. Suddenly he remembered Jamie. He ran up the stairs and Sammy chased him and tried to find a way between his legs.

As Brian ran he screamed. 'Jamie! Jamie! Where are you?'

He looked in each of the bedrooms.

Jamie wasn't in any of them.

He kicked at the bathroom door.

It was empty.

All the time Brian continued to scream out his teenage son's name.

He chased down the stairs, tripped over Sammy and crashed down the last six stairs landing in the hall amongst yet more damage and destruction. He picked himself up and ignoring the cuts on his arms and face walked back into the lounge and sat on the settee and tried to take in the wanton destruction around him. In the silence he heard footsteps crushing the gravel beneath the front window. Sammy immediately broke into a frenzy and raced around the room. Brian rushed into the kitchen grabbed a carving knife and crept back into the lounge and waited. Suddenly open tins of paint crashed through the window adding more layers of wet gloss on top of the already damaged furniture. The chaos was followed by an eerie silence. Sammy nudged Brian but instinctively knew not to pursue affection and crept off to hide behind the settee.

Brian looked furtively around the room so he could identify any obstacles before he reached across and turned off the table light. He stood poised in the darkness in the centre of the lounge with the kitchen knife in one hand and a table leg in the other.

He could feel his heart racing as he stood in the silence and waited.

The heard a sound coming from the kitchen. The door handle was being shaken and the door pushed.

In the darkness Brian picked his way carefully across the lounge and hid behind the door that led into the kitchen. He could hear the door being pushed once more until it suddenly gave way. Brian tensed, clutched the table leg, tightened his grip on the knife and raised it high above his head.

The door swung open, Brian dropped the table leg and grabbed the intruder by the throat.

'It's me . . . Jamie . . .' he said forcing out each breathless word.

Brian released his cast iron grip.

'Sorry, d . . . d . . . dad . . . I had your charger . . .' said Jamie crying out with shock.

When he saw that his father was clutching the carving knife his face drained of all colour.

Brian lowered the knife.

Jamie tried to take it all in.

'Wha . . . ?' he said finding it hard to get out any words. When he had regained his breath he screamed out uncontrollably. 'What the hell happened?' He looked around and tried to take in the extent of the damage before he spoke again. 'Did you do this, dad?'

'Course not . . . we had visitors,' said Brian. Still holding the knife he held his son tightly in his arms. 'Jamie, thank God you're safe'.

'I'm fine, dad . . .' sighed Jamie. 'I'm fine . . .'

Sammy now barked but in a very different way.

'At least they didn't hurt Sammy . . . and it's a good job your mother and Jenny weren't here,' said Brian.

'Have you phoned the police, dad?' asked Jamie.

'No, the bastards ripped the 'phone out of the wall and my mobile's not charged . . . I lost the charger'.

'I know that's why I've come back. I picked up *your* charger'. Jamie held it up and tried to pass it to Brian.

Brian ignored him. Instead he placed the carving knife on the mantlepiece and picked up the pieces of glass and threw it into the corner of the room. 'Come on let's get this cleared up,' he said as he wiped the black paint on his hands in his trousers. 'Be careful . . . some of the paint is still wet'.

There was a sudden crash of breaking glass on the other side of the house.

A brick smashed through the kitchen window followed by a second brick through the glass door.

'Who's doing this, dad?' asked Jamie. 'I can't believe it'.

'You've gotta believe it son. But what makes it so sad is that these people used to work for me'.

'But, dad, I thought all your men were really good. You've always said how nice they were'.

'Do you ever really know anyone, son?' asked his father.

They lifted the plasma television from the floor and stacked it in the corner along with the video and DVD player.

'Put the kettle on, Jamie,' said Brian.

'I wonder if they damaged that?' asked Jamie.

'No . . . they seemed to have ignored the kitchen,' said Brian. He cursed and a wry smile crossed his face. 'Well . . .' He looked around. 'That was until a few minutes ago'.

Jamie filled the kettle and turned it on. Within a few short minutes it was boiling and he opened the fridge to get the milk. He let out an almighty scream, which reverberated around the kitchen.

Brian grabbed the carving knife and rushed in, followed closely by a snarling Sammy. 'What the . . . ?' asked Brian.

Jamie stood holding the fridge door, his face pale and terrified. 'Look in there . . . d . . . d . . .' his voice faded.

Brian reached forward and looked inside.

Their cat had been murdered and mutilated. Its body and entrails had been stuffed amongst the food.

'Alright, son . . . you go back in the lounge and sit down, take Sammy with you. I'll take care of this'. He swore under his breath.

Brian pulled the still bleeding carcass of the cat from the fridge, placed it in a bin liner and tied it. He then removed everything else from the fridge, filled a second bin liner and threw it in the rubbish bin outside.

Brian took two cans of beer from the cold box and handed one to Jamie. 'There you are son, first time eh?'

Jamie looked at him and blushed. 'Are you sure, dad? I mean you would have gone ballistic if you knew I'd even sniffed a beer glass before tonight'.

'Well, maybe you've grown up tonight, son'. He lifted the can. 'Cheers'.

They drank like it was their last.

'OK, now let's get this lot sorted'.

Brian unscrewed the remaining legs from the dining table, collected his tool kit from under the stairs and screwed the table top across the kitchen window and then smashed a dining chair and used the seat to block the hole in the broken kitchen door.

Jamie walked into the hall and picked up the unopened post that had been piling up inside the front door for days.

'Dad, you haven't touched that for ages'.

'I don't see a lot of point, with the problems we've got. What good news are we likely to get in the post?'

'You ought to open it, dad. Some of these letters look important'.

'They probably are . . . but first things first,' he finished his can. 'Come on let's have another one'.

'You know what, Jamie; I don't know what I'd do without you, Jenny and Mum. It's so important to have a family . . . you just remember that'. He rubbed the tears from his eyes and wiped his nose.

They opened the second can.

'Do you think they'll come back again, dad?'

'Who knows? Maybe they've had their kicks by now'. He reflected. 'Let's hope so,' he said.

Although Jamie was dead on his feet he continued to help his father and they worked for several hours until the last of the debris was cleared and the room tidied.

Brian reached across and hugged his son tight.

'Thanks, Jamie'.

Jamie smiled a tired smile back at him.

'I don't know what I would have done without you here tonight,' said Brian. He gently tapped Jamie on the shoulder. 'You've got to get some sleep now, son,' said Brian.

'Are you sure, dad?'

'Yeah, you go and get your sleeping bag and get some sleep . . . I'll need you to help me tomorrow. We can't have both us exhausted, can we?'

While Jamie slept on the lounge floor in his sleeping bag

cuddled up with Sammy, Brian continued to strip the areas of defaced wall paper and place it in bin liners.

Jamie was still asleep on the floor when Brian pulled back the curtains and the early morning sun burst through the window. There was a knock at the door and Brian looked at his watch, tapped it and checked it against the paint splattered clock on the wall.

It was 7:10 am.

He picked up the carving knife and held it behind his back as he opened the door.

'Mr Chapman . . . ? Brian Chapman?' asked the tallest of the two strangers.

'Yes,' answered Brian taken aback. 'Who are you?'

'We represent Accord Finance Company'.

'I understand the vehicles outside are on lease from my clients'.

'You're repo men?'

The men ignored him. Brian looked over the tallest man's shoulder at Sylvia's Micra and the battered Audi that a few short weeks earlier had been his pride and joy.

'Yes, I believe they are,' said Brian. 'But I'm not totally sure'.

'That's all I need to know'. The tall man held out his hand. 'Keys?'

Brian looked across at the table near the door. 'Well, yes . . .'

The man walked across and grabbed the keys.

'Thank you very much'.

'What do you mean thank you very much? What do you think you're doing?'

Sammy joined Brian at the door and nuzzled the tall man.

He kicked out at him; the dog yelped and ran back to Jamie.

'We're repossessing the cars. Your company's gone down, and there's no way you can pay? Is there mate?' he sneered. He shrugged his shoulders, threw one set of keys to the second man and they walked down the drive. While the shortest man started Sylvia's car the tall man dragged open the door of Brian's Audi and they both raced off.

Brian stood in the kitchen and gazed out of the window into the garden. The table and chairs were still on the patio and Brian remembered the last time the family had sat at the table and eaten. Tears welled up in his eyes and he wiped them with his sleeve.

'Morning, dad,' said Jamie wiping the sleep from his eyes as he unlocked the kitchen door and let Sammy out into the back garden.

Brian didn't hear him.

'Hi, dad,' he repeated.

Brian turned around and mumbled. 'Oh hello, Jamie'.

'Do you think we ought to get the 'phone fixed and tell the police?' he asked.

'We should, but I don't see a lot of point. They didn't do anything about the damage at the offices,' he said.

'Don't tell me they wrecked the offices too'. He shook his head wildly. 'What happened?'

Brian nodded and looked dejected. 'It really doesn't matter anymore. Come on, let's go down and see your Nan. See if she'll cook us some breakfast'.

'That'll be nice'.

'Go and get Sammy's lead.

'Sammy's lead? Can't we go in the car?

'Not today, Jamie . . .' he said.

176

Jamie looked at him, confused.

'We're walking.'

Brian grabbed at Jamie's jacket.

'Don't you dare to mention this to your mother.

CHAPTER TWENTY

Green green grass of home

Brian had been brought up in the area and even now only lived a short walk away in houses built in the late sixties and early seventies to satisfy the insatiable demand for post war property. When he was growing up there were still isolated bomb sites, a reminder of the war long gone, a shop on every corner and cars were few and far between. He looked down the road. Cars were parked on both sides of the road clogging up the narrow streets that were never built to accommodate motor vehicles. The corner shops had long gone converted into houses and now everyone made the weekly ritual to the large supermarkets that had sprung up in the fields he'd once played in.

What had happened to the post war innocence and neighbours? He didn't recognise any of them or their cars.

Many of the neighbours had moved away or died.

He thought to himself. *They were old when he lived there.*

Jamie rang the doorbell and Mrs Chapman answered.

'Hello,' she said brightly. 'This is nice . . . to see the two men in my life. I suppose you want me to put the kettle on?'

'Dad, said you'd cook us breakfast,' said Jamie.

'Course I can. Come on in,' she said brightly.

Brian's mother doted on him. He was her only child.

Sammy raced between their legs and stood panting in the kitchen.

Brian sat at the dining table and flicked through the newspaper but didn't read it.

'How's Jenny?' he asked.

'She's fine . . . she's loving it'. She paused. 'It's really nice having her here with me'. She reflected. 'When this is over perhaps she can come and stay more often. She's a wonderful girl, Brian. You and Sylvie are very lucky'.

'What about me, Nan? Am I lovely?' asked Jamie unable to hide his jealousy.

She reached out and gave him a hug.

'Course you are,' she said softly.

Jamie blushed.

'Jenny's playing with Laura next door. They get on like a house on fire,' she said.

She filled the kettle and plugged it in. 'To what do I owe this pleasure?' she asked as she opened the fridge and took out the bacon, sausages and tomatoes.

Brian didn't reply.

She raised her head over the door. 'Can you take some bread out of the bin please, Jamie?'

Jamie opened the bread bin and passed her a handful of sliced white bread.

'Go on, pop it in the toaster then, Jamie, make yourself useful,' she said as she split the bacon and sausages and laid them amongst the sliced tomatoes in the frying pan. She looked down at the dog nuzzling her legs. 'Alright, Sammy, I haven't forgotten you,' she said, as she picked another sausage and slice of bacon from the Tupperware box. She took three eggs from the fridge and placed them delicately in a second frying pan. As soon as the food was cooked she placed the food meticulously onto two large plates, cut up the sausage and bacon for Sammy and placed it on the floor. 'There you are, boy. This is a treat isn't it, Sammy?'

'Come on then you two get stuck in . . .' she said looking at Brian. 'Sammy's got more appetite than you, son,' she said.

Brian sat at the table and looked up at the wedding picture of him and Sylvia in pride of place on the wall. 'Seems like a million years ago,' he said quietly.

'How's Sylvia doing? Is she any better? she asked.

'I called the hospital yesterday. They said she's improving all the time'.

He sipped at his tea.

She looked across at Brian and tilted her head to one side. 'When do you think they'll let us go in and see her?' She paused and thought before she continued. 'Or . . . more importantly when do you think she'll be out?'

Brian shook his head. 'I've no idea . . . she's still under observation. If you'd told me this could ever have happened there's no way I would have ever set up the business . . . .' He smashed his hand on the table and the cups and spoons rattled in the saucers.

Clearly frightened by Brian's uncharacteristic outburst, Jamie jumped and Sammy growled.

His mother coughed and reached gingerly across the worktop and switched on the kettle. 'All right, Brian, I'll make a fresh pot of tea'.

Jamie finished his food and now had his eyes on his father's.

'Has dad told you what happened last night?' he asked.

'No?' replied Mrs Chapman.

Brian elbowed Jamie hard in the ribs but it was too late.

Mrs Chapman placed her tea on the table and she stared hard at Jamie. '*What* happened?' she asked expectantly.

Jamie couldn't hide his misplaced excitement. 'Well, when I got in last night'. He couldn't speak as he remembered the damage. He paused briefly, gathered his thoughts and then continued. 'The lounge . . . you should have seen it . . . video broken and DVD flattened, furniture ripped apart. They even smashed the new TV . . . and . . . they threw paint all over the furniture and sprayed the walls—'

'Is that right, Brian? Have you told the police?'

'No . . . but I will. I'm just trying to get my thoughts together. I'll go to the police station later'.

'I thought you would have done that already . . . made it a priority . . . let them catch the so and so's,' she said angrily.

'They ripped the 'phone out of the wall, Nana,' said Jamie.

Mrs Chapman looked at Brian not knowing how to react. This sort of thing was alien to her. 'It never happened in my days; we could leave the front door open and go out . . . no need to worry about anything like that . . . I hope they catch the hooligans'.

Jamie stabbed at the last sausage on Brian's plate and ate it.

Mrs Chapman looked across at Jamie. 'Why don't you take Sammy for a walk down the park? Eh . . . Jamie?'

Jamie reluctantly stood up and grabbed Sammy and walked towards the door but stopped suddenly. 'You will be all right won't you, dad?'

Brian sucked heavily for breath. 'Yeah . . . course I will. Do as your Nan says and take Sammy for a run . . .' He raised his arm and pointed towards the door. 'Go on. Just be careful and don't go near anyone from work, I don't care who it is,' said Brian. He looked at his watch. 'I'll meet you back here at two . . . on the dot, I don't want to have to worry about you as well,' he said.

'Thanks, Nan. Come on Sammy . . . Walkies!" he said as he picked up the lead.

Jamie kissed his Nan and she hugged him in her arms. 'You're growing now, Jamie, nearly as tall as your Father,' she said proudly.

Jamie put Sammy on the lead and they raced out of the house.

'He's a lovely lad, Brian, just like you were when you were his age'. She looked across at the school photo of Brian. 'You're very lucky,' she said. She picked up the plates and put them in the bowl. 'I expect you want another one, eh Brian?' she said holding up his mug. She emptied the tea leaves into the sink and stood looking out of the window waiting for the kettle to boil. The kettle clicked off and she poured the boiling water into the tea pot and sat down with Brian at the table.

'Come on then Brian. What on earth is going on? And what's this about a break-in at home?'

She sat staring at him and waited.

Brian looked away from her and stood up.

'Has this got anything to do with the business?' she asked.

He nodded slowly and looked into space.

'It's been a liability from day one . . .' He faked a smile. 'And do you know what makes it worse? It's the guys thinking that *we* were making all the money'. He raised his voice. 'But in reality they're the ones who couldn't lose. And I tell you this . . . none of them . . . not *one* would *ever* consider taking the chances me and Sylve did!'

She moved close to him and put her arms around him.

He looked at her his tearful eyes about to release the emotion. 'I'm afraid it is'. He nodded. 'Yeah, things are getting worse all right, they came and took my car away this morning,' he said.

'They what?' she said.

'Two repo men came, knocked on the door . . . and asked for the keys, got in the cars . . . mine and Sylvie's'. He took a deep breath, rubbed the stubble on his chin and sighed. '. . . and drove 'em away'.

'That's never right? They can't do that!' His mother said angrily.

She took the lid off the tea pot, stirred at it blindly and immediately poured it.

Brian looked back at her. 'They can . . . and they did! Mind you it won't be worth much . . . ,' he said with a forced smile.

'How are you going to get about now, Brian? You still need to get out to the office, don't you?'

'I do, but not for much longer. The girls, Pam and Jackie, are coming in to help but there's not a lot for them to do anymore'. He laughed. 'And Eric, you remember him?'

She smiled. 'Um . . . course I do'.

'Well, he's been great. A big surprise and the girls are working for nothing'.

Mrs Chapman opened her handbag, took out an old black wallet and counted out some of the notes and handed them to Brian. 'There you are'.

Brian blushed and shook his head wildly. 'I can't take any more, mum. I've already got you into a mess, with the seventy thousand you let me have'.

'That's alright, don't worry about that. Everything will sort itself out,' she said.

He reflected before speaking. 'I suppose it will'.

She forced the money into his hand. 'Go on take it. Find yourself a runabout. It'll do until you get back on your feet.'

Reluctantly Brian took the money and made to stand.

'On no you don't, son'.

He found it hard to hide his embarrassment and lowered his head.

She smiled. 'You haven't finished your tea,' she said pushing the mug towards him.

Brian smiled back. 'Oh!' He picked up the mug and emptied it. 'I tell you what, mum, as well as all this,' he held up the money, 'you make a great cup of tea'.

'There you are, son . . . You smiled. It's not the end of the world. Remember . . . there's always someone else worse off than you'. She pointed her finger at him as she spoke. 'Don't you forget it,' she said.

'Thanks mum'.

He stood up and as they hugged each other they both tried to hide their tears.

CHAPTER TWENTY-ONE

Money makes the world go 'round

Brian walked up and down the back street car lot looking at the vehicles for sale. The cheapest car was a Vauxhall Astra at two hundred and fifty pounds.

The salesman slid out of his office to meet Brian. 'Morning mate . . . that's a lovely runner'. He pointed at a BMW. 'Just needs a bit of work and it'll go on forever'.

Brian didn't react.

'I tell ya what . . . you can have it for two grand'.

Brian squeezed the notes in his pocket.

The salesman guided Brian to an old Volvo. 'What about this one? I can let you drive it away today for?' He feigned deliberation. 'Let's say eighteen hundred,' he said as he smiled at Brian.

'I don't think so,' said Brian as he walked away.

'I can see you drive a hard bargain. How much *do you* wanna pay?' he asked.

Brian looked at him blankly. 'I've no idea. But what I do know is that car sales are at rock bottom . . . never been worse since the scrappage nonsense came and went'.

The car salesman looked at him, screwed up his face and nodded. 'Um . . . OK, so what sort of car are you looking for? What do you want it for?'

Brian looked at him and slowly shook his head.

'To drive . . . nothing more'.

The car salesman smiled.

'I see . . . so you're not really fussed'.

Brian shook his head and walked across to the pale green battered Vauxhall Astra.

'Do you fancy that one mate?' he asked, opening the driver's door. 'That's a tidy motor, MOT and taxed . . . you can drive it away for two hundred and fifty quid'.

Brian took the notes from his pocket, turned away and counted them. 'I'll tell you what. I'll give you one hundred and eighty . . . cash'.

'Done!' said the salesman as he reached out his hand.

Brian ignored it and slid one twenty pound note into his trouser pocket and counted out the rest into the salesman's hand.

'If you wanna come into the office and I'll let yer have the log book and MOT certificate'.

Brian slipped the documents in his pocket and walked back to the car.

'Oh, by the way, mate, I should get to the garage sharpish and fill her up, she's in the red . . . on empty'.

Brian shot him a look of indifference and pulled away.

Brian sat in his mother's kitchen drinking a mug of tea and Sammy rushed in followed by Jamie.

'Hi, dad . . . I see you're back'. He took off his jacket. 'That's not *our* car outside is it?' he asked as he shot Brian a look of disgust. 'It's not . . . is it?'

Brian looked up at him. 'Yep, that's ours'.

'Has it got a fifth gear?' asked Jamie.

'It's only just about got four,' said Brian. He paused. 'But it'll get us around for a while'.

Jamie looked around. 'Where's, Nan?'

'Gone to get her pension'.

Brian bent down and stroked Sammy. 'I'm going in a minute but do you want a cup of tea?'

'No thanks, dad, but you can drop me at Richard's?'

The vast tarmac car park that had been completely deserted earlier was now filling rapidly and a line of queuing cars choked the nearby roads causing near chaos for other road users. In the heavy rain and strong winds, the impatient drivers eventually began to pull in, and fought to fill the spaces nearest to the main building. The occupants rushed out of their cars and joined the ever-growing crowd, pushing their way towards the double doors.

Brian drove into the car park braked hard and blocked the entrance. He pushed himself hard back into the seat and in sheer disbelief, shook his head violently, as he tried to take in the chaotic scenes around him. At the same time, he tried desperately to keep the engine ticking over, dropped the clutch and teased the accelerator pedal. Unable to hold back his feelings any longer he screamed angrily, the deafening roar reverberating around the car. 'Bloody leeches, they didn't waste any sodding time!'

His lapse in concentration caused the car to shudder to a

standstill and it took several attempts before the engine turned over and he was finally able to make his way into the car park. He drove around frantically until he found the only remaining free bay at the far side of the car park near to the group of vans that were now surrounded by people. As he manoeuvred into the space, he scratched a shiny black BMW parked to his left. His car stalled and he sat looking out through the dirty and cracked windscreen. He tried desperately to calm down, oblivious to the damage he had inflicted on the adjacent vehicle.

Finding it extremely difficult to breathe he fumbled in the pockets of his jacket until he found his Ventolin inhaler. Pulling it from his pocket, he pushed it between his narrow lips and squeezed it several times before the effects of the drug took effect. He moved awkwardly across to the passenger seat and pushed open the door. Realising that he did not have enough room to squeeze out of the car, he reluctantly climbed back over the gear stick and hand brake into the driver's seat. He searched the glove compartment until he found the broken window winder, held it in place with his left hand while he wound down the window and then reached for the outside door handle. The rusty and dented door creaked loudly as he tried in vain to push it open. Getting more frustrated, he slid down into the seat, pushed his shoulder against the door until it swung forcefully into the van parked alongside it, the impact denting the bodywork.

Relieved, he now stood in the car park beside his car looking strangely out of place compared to the other drivers who were now making their way excitedly towards the building. As he walked between the dirty commercial vehicles he subconsciously ran his finger down the side of the nearest van to reveal unblemished navy blue paintwork. Noticing the result of his effort, he took a dirty handkerchief from his jacket pocket and worked energetically rubbing the dirt to reveal the clean grey signwriting along the side of the van. He turned to the next vehicle, whose bodywork was severely dented and looked close to a write off. He checked the registration and realised it was Colin Corke's new van. Overcome with emotion he choked back the tears, kicked at the tyres and slowly walked blindly towards the front entrance. With his back bent and his narrow shoulders drooping forward, he picked his way between the last row of cars, stopping only for a brief moment to look up at the crookedly nailed, hand painted sign – Auction today.

Bending his head even lower, he stooped unnecessarily, and walked through the entrance.

The large crowd had already assembled inside the building, were packed tightly together, in what was previously the general office. Desks, chairs, filing cabinets, computers and all manner of office equipment were marked with a Lot number and spread all around the office. Mr Fitzgerald the bespectacled middle aged auctioneer stood, on a makeshift platform, a foot or so above them and checked to see that anyone interested in the auction was inside. After clearing his throat, he began. 'Lot one – a four drawer filing cabinet. Let's start the bidding at twenty pounds'.

In the front of the crowd, a young man shyly waved his catalogue while the auctioneer looked around the room for other interest. Although an overweight man joined in the bidding, at sixty-five pounds, he lost interest, allowing the younger man to complete the purchase and to smile nervously at the people nearest to him.

During the bidding for the first item, Brian pushed his way

unnoticed around the perimeter of the crowd. Finding a place in a dark corner, he removed a small notebook and pen from his inside pocket and began to write down the price of every item as it was sold.

Three hours later a hoarse but much-relieved auctioneer found his second wind and in a raised voice, he continued, 'ladies and gentlemen, the penultimate item of the day Lot 427.

The young assistant raised a fax machine above his head and the auctioneer continued. 'This is a very sophisticated piece of equipment,' he lied. 'What am I bid?' The crowd had dwindled to only a few small groups of people who had little interest in the last item. Many of the people chuckled to themselves at the auctioneer's outright exaggeration.

Pam stood with Jackie and nervously raised her hand. 'Thirty pounds!' she said.

Brian stood in the shadows and cursed under his breath as the auctioneer looked around the room and repeated the figure again. 'Thirty pounds, do I hear thirty five?'

Eric, raised his hand, but Pam, after hesitating for a split second, continued to bid.

On the podium, the auctioneer sensed that the battle was almost over. 'Ninety five pounds, am I bid one hundred?' He looked around the room but the interest had now diminished. 'Going once, going twice'. He raised his hand and smashed the gavel onto the desk.

Ladies and gentlemen, this is the last lot of the day. His clerk held up a cardboard box of assorted items. He dipped in his hand and pulled out the inlaid letter opener.

Brian froze and fell back against the wall.

'Sylvia gave me that,' he murmured. He couldn't look and

lowered his head in shame. He wanted to rush up and grab it but was transfixed and rooted to the spot.

'The last Lot of the day . . . sold for three pounds'. Pam smiled and walked towards the auctioneer's clerk.

Brian winced and trembled with anger. *Three pounds he thought.*

'Ladies and gentlemen that concludes today's auction. I would like to thank you on behalf of the Liquidators and would remind you that any items purchased today, must be paid for and removed within the next hour. There will be a number of auctions of a similar nature in the next few days and I would suggest that you review the local press; our web site; or telephone our office'. He forced a tired smile. 'Thank you'.

Brian remained in the corner and concentrated on totalling the figures, the remaining members of the public moved towards the clerk to pay for the items that they had bought.

Shaking his head, Brian mumbled to himself. 'Six thousand, five hundred and twenty four pounds and fifty sodding pence, that's not going to go very bloody far'.

Brian pushed the notebook and pen into his pocket and walked through the remaining empty and deserted offices. Looking into the last office he noticed a photograph on the floor behind the glazed door and bent down to pick it up, but as he stopped to look at it the auctioneer's assistant walked into the room and confronted him. 'Can I help you, mate? What are you doing in here?' he asked angrily.

Brian tried to hide the photograph behind his back. 'It's alright, it belongs to me'.

'I think you must be mistaken, sir?' questioned the auctioneer's assistant.

'No . . . it is mine. I'm just having one last look ar . . .' mumbled Brian in response to his interrogator.

'Oh yeah . . . you are . . . are you?' the auctioneer's assistant smiled falsely, humouring him.

Brian replied in an almost inaudible voice. 'I'm . . .' He cleared his throat and continued. 'I'm . . . I'm Brian Chapman'.

The auctioneer's assistant was taken aback and continued to stare, and not totally sure that the stranger was telling the truth, continued to interrogate him. 'So you're . . . Brian Chapman eh?'

The stranger nodded, gave a forced smile, handed him the photograph and pointed at a smartly dressed man in the centre. The auctioneer's assistant cast his eye over the scruffy man standing in front of him. He studied the photograph more closely for a few seconds and finally satisfied with the man's explanation handed it back to him'.

'Nice offices, it's a pity we didn't get more for this stuff and your vans. Mind you'. He paused. 'Yours is the ninth this week, you can't give anything away these days'.

Brian stared at him, while he felt in his pocket for his notebook. 'I know,' he said.

He gave a half smile, turned and walked out of the room, and down the corridor that had been his pride and joy for the last thirteen years. He stopped walking, and glanced briefly at the photograph that had been taken only a few months earlier at the annual company dinner. He mumbled to himself. 'Those were the days'.

He took one last look around the office and as he felt the tears welling up, walked slowly towards the main doors.

The auctioneer's assistant called after him. 'Bye, Mr Chapman'.

Without any acknowledgement or response, Brian walked out of the building.

Now standing alone, he pulled the filthy handkerchief from his pocket and wiped his eyes.

He took a deep breath, straightened his back and walked slowly across the now deserted car park towards his car.

The grey sky darkened and the rain laden clouds driven on by the strong south westerly wind built up above him and it started to rain heavily. Still clutching the rolled up photograph, he ran towards his car and he made a pathetic attempt to protect himself from the elements by pulling his narrow jacket collar up around his neck.

An ear-splitting shot reverberated across the car park and the photograph, propelled by the gust of wind, blew out of Brian's hand as he slipped and fell to the ground.

The company sign, split in two by the strong wind, bounced across the car park and flew into the air.

Brian rose slowly to his feet and watched in silence as and sign crashed into the side of his Astra.

A terrified Sammy pawed at the window.

'Alright, boy, take it easy,' he said as he opened the rear door and let the relieved Sammy jump up and nuzzle him.

'Come on boy . . . let's get away from all this'.

Brian drove out of the car park in a state of shock and total dismay.

CHAPTER TWENTY-TWO

Don't call me angel

Brian pressed the intercom and the door clicked open. He walked up to reception and the same middle aged woman appeared at the window and slid it open.

'Hello again, Mr Chapman,' she said. She stopped and looked him up and down before she continued. 'How are *you* feeling?' she asked.

Brian nodded. 'I'm fine . . . just a little tired,' he said softly.

'Um . . . Well.' She smiled back at him. 'We have good news for you'.

Brian forced a smile.

'Mrs Chapman seems to be responding to her medication . . . and Doctor Thompson is very happy with the change'.

'Will she know me now?' gushed Brian.

The receptionist replied immediately and smiled for the first time. 'I think you may be pleasantly surprised'. She paused. 'But there's still a long way to go . . . Take it slowly, Mr Chapman. Be patient . . . Please'.

Brian waited for the Asian nurse to escort him to the canteen and he saw Sylvia sitting at the window reading a magazine.

'Hello, Sylvia,' said Brian.

She looked up from her book and beamed at him.

'Hello, it's so nice to see you'. She said. She tapped the nearest chair. 'Come and tell me all the news'.

Brian sat in a chair on the opposite side of the table and leaned towards her.

She didn't flinch.

Brian had to think quickly. *He couldn't tell her anything that had happened. He knew it would destroy her.*

'Well . . . we're all fine and the kids send their love and can't wait to see you,' he said.

Did she know him?

He stood up.

'Shall I make us a coffee?' he asked.

'That would be nice,' she replied softly.

Brian walked over to the kitchen area and took two mugs from the dishwasher. He made the coffee and returned to the table.

She gave him a peculiar look.

He suddenly remembered and returned to the dishwasher took out a plastic beaker and poured Sylvia's coffee into it.

'There you are . . . sorry about that,' he said.

She gave him a warm smile.

'Let's go in the activity room . . . I do my relaxation in there . . . It's quiet . . . I like that . . . Do you want me read one of poems? They just keep coming . . . I can't believe it . . . me writing poems . . . I wanted a small house—'

'Why?' asked Brian.

'To be on our own . . .' She had to think before speaking again. 'I mean all of us'. She counted the names off on her fingers as she said them. 'Jenny, Jamie and Brian . . .'

She laughed to herself and tapped her fingers. 'Ah . . . and Sammy'. She laughed innocently. 'Mustn't forget dear, Sammy'. She sipped from the plastic beaker. 'We need to find some space of our own . . . I don't know . . . a small house . . .' she looked blankly across the room. 'All I can remember is seeing the doctor and then this man came and told me he would help me to find a new house . . .' She turned to Brian and looked directly into his face but clearly didn't know him. 'I'm not ill . . . I fell down the stairs . . . Do you know . . . ?' Her voice faded to nothing and she didn't complete her question.

She waited for Brian to answer her.

He nodded to her to continue and sipped at his coffee.

She didn't continue.

He looked at her intently and smiled.

'Well . . . yesterday . . .' Sylvia paused before pointing across the room at the large overweight woman and continued. 'She . . .' She stopped and covered her mouth before speaking between her fingers. 'She stood up and peed herself. It was pouring out onto the carpet. I told the nurse and when she approached her she punched her in the mouth . . . It was my fault . . . I thought she was going to punch me. They held her down and gave her an injection . . .' She reflected. 'Can you believe that?' She pointed at the mysterious stains on the carpet. 'Right there, she did it . . .'

Brian looked down at the soiled carpet.

'It's been cleaned up now,' she said.

Brian sipped at his coffee once again.

'Do you want me to read one of my poems?' she asked.

'Yes please,' said Brian.

'I want to go to France . . . Be on our own for a while

. . . Brian, Jenny, Jamie and Sammy . . . everyone,' she said excitedly.

Brian looked at her sadly. *Did she recognise him?*

'When I come out we're all getting a small house . . . nothing flash. Get some space of our own. They'll all understand . . . I can't believe they will . . . but *they* will. I just need to sort my head out . . . They'll help me. I couldn't get away from anything, the business . . . I wanted to . . .' She hesitated. 'To have a rest . . . Do you know we've have only used the boat three times in the last year?

'Sell it,' said Brian. 'Get rid of it. Let's just sell it,' he lied.

They didn't own a boat.

'I have . . . I mean I will when I get out of here'. She pulled up her sleeves. 'Look at this rash . . . they've given me,' she tilted her head to one side and thought long and hard. '. . . anti-his . . .' She rubbed at her face as an inane smile crossed her face. 'That's right . . . anti-histamines . . .' she yelped excitedly. 'Yeah, they'll get rid of it and then . . .' She screwed up her face before looking back at Brian wide eyed. 'And then . . . I'll be alright again'.

Brian nervously returned her smile and then lowered his head. He looked directly at the thick scars on both wrists and shook his head in disbelief. He knew they would always be there but he tried to forget as much as he could of what had happened that horrendous night.

She pointed at his mug. 'How's the coffee?'

'Fine . . . very nice,' replied Brian.

'I'll go and get my poems'.

Brian made to follow her.

'No! You can't come'. She gave him a fierce look. 'We're not allowed to have *visitors* in our room'.

Brian sipped his coffee and watched as Sylvia; *his wife*, shuffled out of the room.

Was all this his fault?

Sylvia returned with several crumpled sheets of off-white paper and sat down at a different table.

Brian looked across at her.

'Would you like to read me a poem?'

'That would be lovely,' she said.

'Can I sit with you,' asked Brian.

'Yes . . . Come on,' she said excitedly.

She pointed at the furthest chair. 'Sit here'.

She read her first poem. It didn't scan and was infantile. 'Do you like that one? Listen to this . . . And this . . .' She read several more poems of a similar style and all of them were on the same subject: *Freedom*.

'They're very good,' lied Brian.

'Do you really like them?'

'Yeah . . . they're good . . . better than anything I could write. I wrote poems when I was in hospital in Germany . . . I was very lonely . . . I think the change of environment helps you to do it'.

'Listen to this one . . .' she said excitedly. 'It's not quite finished yet'. She turned the page and read yet another poem that was almost identical to the previous four.

Brian couldn't control his feelings any longer. He turned away and stood up.

The discordant singing could be heard in the day room.

Sylvia stood up, tapped him on the shoulder and smiled at him. 'Shall we go and sing?' she asked excitedly.

Brian followed Sylvia down the corridor keeping a few feet behind her as she shuffled along amongst the other patients, heading in the same direction, who seemed to be entranced by the percussive sounds coming from the room along the corridor.

The large room with its high ceilings and decorative rooflights was incredibly bright and airy. Pictures painted by past and present residents covered almost every inch of the wall space many of which were now faded by the sun and torn by jealous or angry residents still had a place for the time being. The wooden chairs had been arranged in a semi-circle around an area where the musicians had set up on their own brightly coloured rug. Brian was surprised to see male patients for the first time and they all sat on one side of the room. He watched as male and female patients sat in their own invisible zones.

Sylvia guided Brian towards the male section, pointed at a chair and left to sit with the female patients.

Several of the nurses and carers sat amongst the patients and waited while the entertainers moved amongst them and handed everyone percussion of some sort. Sylvia was handed a pair of maracas and Brian was given a tambourine which had a ripped skin and only a few zils left on it. As soon as everyone had some sort of instrument the female leader of the group welcomed everyone and the group began to play their series of simple songs and nursery rhymes. The atmosphere was totally different to anything Brian had seen during his frequent visits and he watched as Sylvia smiled and joined in with every song. The enthusiasm soon rubbed off on him and he played his tambourine with renewed vigour and for a short time he lost himself in the moment. Exactly fifty seven minutes from the start of their performance the female leader looked towards the guitarist and while he played the chords she thanked everyone for coming. Everyone clapped enthusiastically and began to sing the old Appalachian tune 'Coming 'round the mountains.' For two minutes they raised the roof and sang at the top of their voices. Suddenly there was silence and after they reluctantly handed back their instruments they filed out of the room.

Brian waited for most of the patients to leave before he moved across to the leader of the group and handed her the tambourine. He eyed her tightly plaited purple hair and piercings in her nose and top lip but as he got nearer to her those young girlish looks were replaced by the results of the many years of her much earlier sixties hippy lifestyle. Although she had maintained her teenage figure her tired eyes and heavily lined face showed that she was at least twenty years older than he had first thought.

He eyed her closely before speaking.

'Do you enjoy what you do here?' he asked.

She looked Brian up and down and thought hard before she answered. She stared directly into Brian's eyes and spoke softly. 'I didn't at first'. She paused and remembered that time. 'Do you know there is a way of singing so that tears won't interfere with what you're there to do?'

Brian gave her a puzzled look.

She ignored him and continued. 'You have to learn how to isolate your thoughts and feelings.' She smiled thoughtfully. 'When I was growing up our music and drama teachers would send us to the local hospice to practice before going in front of what they termed a 'real' audience. Enid, my best friend, looked out at all the pale, gaunt faces attached by tubes to various life-supporting machines, smelt that unmistakable odour of decay and antiseptic, and rushed out of the room'.

The woman straightened up and flicked her plaited hair. 'I never had that problem. I would focus on the more healthy ones and pretend the others were just making faces and as I grew older the denial slowly grew less and less. Now, no matter how much I am affected by patients, I can still sing'.

Brian tried to understand but continued to look at her blankly.

She continued. 'Although most of the people *here* have mental health issues they do look forward to us coming to sing and entertain them'. She smiled at Brian. 'For many it's the highlight of their week'.

Brian nodded his agreement enthusiastically.

They were temporally distracted by a woman screaming and thrashing out in the corner.

'Um.' She turned back to Brian. 'Well then there are the hopeless ones who hate being with others and the nurses have to remove them from the room as quick as they can or the whole group will deteriorate into total bedlam'. She paused as she realized she had used an inappropriate word.

'Doesn't it upset you when they get upset?' he asked.

She looked around at the patients shuffling out of the room and smiled again. 'There are many reasons for patients crying or shouting out but it is a fantastic and unimaginable emotion when music reaches places that haven't been touched in a long while . . .'

'I know.' Brian nodded to her sympathetically.

She coughed and exposed her pierced tongue and subconsciously flicked it between her lips before she continued to speak. 'It's difficult to know which songs will work and which songs to avoid so we tend to go with the safe ones and perform them in the same order each week'.

Brian nodded. 'They seemed to enjoy it.' He paused and smiled. 'And so did I—'

He was interrupted as another woman hummed tunelessly and waved her arms around ceremoniously as though she was conducting the invisible silence.

The leader looked across at the woman and smiled. 'And as you can see they love to join in with us . . .'

Sylvia moved towards Brian and tapped him on the shoulder. It was the first time she had actually touched him since she left home in the ambulance.

'Will you come again?' she asked. She looked up at him innocently and with a fixed smile on her face waited for his answer.

He replied with the widest of smiles. 'Of course I will,' he said. 'It will be my pleasure . . .'

Sylvia handed her maracas to the leader, dropped her head and followed everyone else towards the door.

The group leader watched Sylvia walk up the corridor before she turned back to Brian. 'Family?' she asked.

Brian nodded as he pushed his wedding ring around his finger. 'My wife,' he mumbled.

'She will get better, but you need to be patient.' She smiled. 'And as long as she takes her medication she'll be back to normal in a matter of weeks.'

Brian's demeanour suddenly changed. 'Normal? How can she get back to normal? You saw her?'

'Well . . . What I meant was that she . . . your wife, will gradually get better and then all you need is time and . . . on your part . . . patience'.

CHAPTER TWENTY-THREE

Things can only get better

Jamie was cooking the toast when there was a knock at the front door. He flicked the switch and turned the toaster off before answering the door. A middle aged, rotund man with ruddy complexion and thinning hair, carrying a battered briefcase, stood on the top step immediately in front of him. Standing quietly behind him was a much younger man in a navy blue pin striped suit. 'Good morning, Mr Chapman please,' said the suited man.

'Who wants him?' asked Jamie.

'Mr Baber,' replied the rotund man sternly.

Jamie turned and shouted up the stairs. 'Dad, someone to see you!'

Brian was shaving and shouted back. 'Who is it, Jamie?'

'Mr Baber to see you, dad'.

'Who?' asked Brian.

He walked down the stairs, shaving foam covering his face and a towel around his neck.

'Brian Chapman, can I help?'

Mr Baber spoke. 'Mr Chapman, I'm a bailiff and I have

a repossession order issued by the County Court, which gives me authority to repossess this property on behalf of the Southbourne Building Society. You are permitted to remove any personal belongings you wish to take with you'.

'Wh . . . ?' mouthed Brian.

He stood looking at them unable to speak.

Jamie joined him at the door and looked down at the unopened letters piled up against the door.

'Dad, I told you, you should have opened them,' he said kicking at the letters.

'I'm afraid many of these problems could be avoided but people who have defaulted on their mortgages, or owe a lot of money, tend to ignore letters until it's too late,' said the suited man.

Brian looked over their shoulders and parked at the end of the drive was a bright yellow van with the letters 'C and P Property Services.' The driver and passenger both wearing grey overalls left the vehicle and walked around to the side of the van; slid back the doors removed their tool boxes and slammed the doors closed.

The two tradesmen then walked up the drive and for the first time Brian recognised Craig Jameson and Colin Corke.

Before Brian could say anything the bailiff spoke.

'Mr Chapman, if you could gather your possessions together, these gentlemen will change the door locks,' he said pointing at Craig and Colin.

Brian found it hard to control his anger but Jamie pulled him inside.

'Come on, dad, we've got to get as much as we can and don't forget mum's jewellery and our passports . . . things like that'.

Brian turned to Jamie.

'Already done it . . . left them at your Nan's'. Brian stopped in mid-sentence and his demeanour suddenly changed and he turned to the bailiff. 'How long have we got?' he said softly.

The bailiff looked at his watch and turned to the suited man. 'Shall we say . . . ten minutes?

The suited man nodded.

Despite his show of bravado, Craig stood nervously behind the bailiff.

'Start with the back door locks,' boomed the bailiff. 'And sitex up all the windows!'

Brian reacted immediately and reached out to grab Craig but couldn't force his way between the bailiff and the suited man. 'Keep that bastard out of my house 'til I've gone or I swear I'll kill him!' he screamed.

'Is that a threat, Mr Chapman?' asked the bailiff?'

Craig sneered at him.

Jamie grabbed at Brian's arm and pulled him inside. 'Come on dad, we're wasting time'.

Brian pushed Jamie's arm away.

'I want this place totally secure,' said the bailiff.

'By the time we've finished even that sad bastard Chapman won't be able to get in,' bragged Craig gloating as he drilled into the lock.

Brian raged.

Craig stopped drilling and turned to face him. 'Do you like the van, Brian?'

Brian's whole body stiffened.

Craig smirked at him inanely and as he spoke stretched each word. 'C and P services . . . Craig . . . and . . . Pam—'

'You bastard!' screamed Brian.

'What's happening, dad?'

'Throwing us out onto the street . . . the bastar . . . !' he screamed wildly.

'They can't do that!' shrieked Jamie.

Brian dragged Jamie inside. 'Come on, Jamie! Pack a few things and I'll drop you at your Nan's'.

Jamie looked at him, his eyes glazed and confused. 'Can they really throw us out, dad?'

'I don't know,' said Brian, shaking his head in total disbelief. 'I just don't know . . . but I'm not going down without a fight,' he mumbled.

While Jamie collected his Wii and electronic games, throwing them into a cardboard box, Brian walked up the stairs and into the bathroom.

A few minutes later Brian arrived at the front door carrying two hurriedly packed bin liners.

Jamie stood looking at him lost for words. 'Wow!' he mouthed.

The bullet headed Brian was clearly a very different person. His head now totally shaven exposed the numerous rugby scars. Everyone was taken totally by surprise and he used the advantage to force his way between the bailiff and the suited man.

Craig and Colin hung back nervously, their bravado suddenly left them as Brian snarled and made to attack them before walking slowly down the drive. He threw the bags in the direction of his car and turned suddenly. He propelled himself into the air and landed immediately in front of Craig. Brian rose with controlled breathing but as he exhaled he let out the loudest roar.

Craig stood motionless as Brian looked directly into his traumatized face.

Brian clenched his fists before he head butted Craig, splitting his nose. Sinew and blood flew in every direction. Brian lunged forward and kicked out wildly his foot landing in Craig's groin before he lashed out with his fists like a man possessed. His powerful well aimed blows to Craig's midriff instantly broke a number of ribs.

Craig screamed with pain and lurched forward. He raised his hands in submission but Brian continued to pummel Craig's body. Craig stumbled backwards across the lawn until he fell into the centre of the rose bed and let out an ear splitting scream of absolute agony. He was trapped. The sharp thorns cut deep and painfully into every part of his soft flesh. The slightest movement causing him to let out screams of sheer agony as the excruciating pain paced through his whole body.

No one stepped forward to help him instead they stood in silence and looked on.

Colin Corke picked up his tools and walked briskly down the drive. He stopped briefly and turned to Craig. 'You're a waste of fucking space!' he raged. He looked towards Brian and the back to Craig. 'You'll never be half the man, Mr Chapman is!' He could feel the anger building up inside him and he screamed out uncontrollably. 'Why did I listen to you . . . you're nothing but a fucking loser!'

Brian grabbed at the bulging bin liners, thrust his head back proudly and with his whole body erect, walked towards the car.

The bailiff and the suited man were close to clapping his performance but held back.

A shocked Jamie stood and looked on before he raced after his father and climbed into the passenger seat.

Colin stood on the pavement and as Brian drove slowly past he mouthed to him. 'Sorry, Mr Chapman'.

Brian acknowledged him with a slow desperate nod.

Mr Baber looked across at Craig, whose face had drained of all colour, and clicked a number on his mobile. Still looking directly at Craig he spoke into his mobile. 'I've got another one for you, George. Can you meet me?' He nodded. 'OK . . . give me a call when you finish up on that one. Bye'. He slipped the mobile into his jacket pocket.

Craig didn't respond. He knew he had lost his most prized client.

A subdued, Mr Baber and the suited man entered the house and began to make an inventory of the contents while they waited for the replacement locksmith to attend.

As Brian drove towards the junction of the main road Jamie let out an almighty yell.

Brian braked hard throwing Jamie towards the windscreen. 'Hang on, dad!'

Brian glared at him. 'What the hell?'

Jamie struggled to gain his breath before he spoke. 'We forgot Sammy!' he screamed.

They drove back to the house and as Jamie ran towards the house Sammy bounded out to meet him and nearly knocked him over as he jumped into the car and out the other side.

Jamie grabbed him, pushed him into the back sea amongst the bin liners and bags, closed the doors and looked around the packed car as he pulled on his seat belt. 'You don't need to worry about dog hairs in *this* car, do you dad?' said Jamie.

Brian flicked the indicator and gave one last look at his

house and then at Sammy panting in the back seat. 'Come on boy,' he said sadly.

Brian drove in silence for several miles before Jamie finally spoke. 'How did you manage that, dad? I didn't think you had it in you'.

'Who the fuck do these people think they are?' raged Brian.

Jamie smiled back at him with a knowing smile and nodded.

Brian ignored him. 'I'm dropping you off at your Nan's. OK'.

'Can I stay with Richard?'

'Course you can.'

Brian continued to drive without speaking.

'I still can't believe you did that, dad,' he said excitedly.

Brian stopped at the traffic lights and reflected. 'Maybe I should have done it a long time ago . . . I thought people would play the game if they were treated right—'

'Dad . . . did you know that Richard's dad went through this is in the last recession? He had a huge company and lost it all'. He smiled at his father. 'He works at home on his own now and he's doing great . . . said he didn't want to have to rely on other people for his future'.

Brian looked hard at him and thought long and hard before speaking. 'Um . . . after all this shit'. He nodded angrily. 'I reckon he's probably got it right. Why employ anybody?'

CHAPTER TWENTY-FOUR

Wishing and hoping

Brian drove to the railway station and parked up. He couldn't lock his car so took his laptop with him walked into the all night station café, ordered a mug of tea and picked up the last sandwich on the shelf and sat at the only empty table. He placed the mug of tea and sandwich next to the laptop and sat looking into the café. Groups of drunks swayed at the counter as they tried to place their orders in nonsensical babble. The young girls behind the counter clearly intimidated by the men were only faintly reassured by the two railway policemen who stood at the door and desperately tried not to make eye contact with the drunks.

Brian switched on the laptop and sat looking out onto the platform. Huge posters advertised the bogus opportunities from banks to lend money to companies and offers of more credit to their current credit card users. He clenched his fists and randomly kicked out at the chairs in front of him. A train pulled into the platform and obscured his view and with it he turned his attention to the carriage doors as they were flung open. Huge piles of bound morning papers direct from London were unloaded from the train onto a series of wire sided trailers and towed up the platform by a motorised vehicle.

Brian thought. *Tomorrow's news: tonight.*

The porter stopped briefly to throw several packs of papers towards the platform café door and talk to the guard before he drove off zig zagging along the platform avoiding the invisible passengers.

Brian watched a grey haired man pick up several bundles of the papers and carry them into the café, cut through the tight cord and carefully place the different papers on the news stand.

Brian walked over and bought his copy. He sat back at his table read and reread the headlines '*1800 homes set to be repossessed in the South West this year.*'

His mind raced back to the previous morning when *his* home had been repossessed. His whole body stiffened with anger and he struggled to breathe. He reached deep into jacket pocket for his inhaler and pulled it out along with his memory stick. With the memory stick still in his hand in utter desperation he forced the Ventolin inhaler between his trembling lips and pumped it frantically. He took huge gulps of the drug and inhaled erratically. The excess drug flowed out of his mouth rising like some heavy smoker exhaling. As he recovered he fiddled with the laptop and opened it, he pushed the mug and pasty aside, pushed in the memory stick and methodically checked the accounts, suppliers and sales ledger.

He stopped abruptly and slurped his now cold tea.

He didn't notice it.

What he'd discovered was totally unbelievable.

He checked and rechecked the figures several times until he knew that what he had discovered was correct.

*

Natasha's flat was difficult to find. He had only visited it once before but he hoped to see Craig's van. He wasn't disappointed and as he made his way slowly along the road he saw it parked tight against the block of flats. The bedroom light was still on, no doubt Natasha was helping Craig to treat his cuts and nurse his dented pride.

Brian drove a few hundred yards down the road and parked his car. He removed his laptop and climbed out of the passenger door because he knew the noise generated by opening the driver's door would be heard by everyone. Sammy lay on the rear seat. He stirred and lifted his head but Brian patted him gently and he settled back on the seat.

Brian walked to Craig's van and broke into it. He pushed it down the slope and let it run into the road until it came to a standstill. He ripped out the cables beneath the steering column, hard wired it and drove off.

Brian wasted no time.

He drove to the company lock up and using Craig's car jack effortlessly smashed his way into the building. He scoured the stores ripped open a plastic bag, took out a woollen *beanie* hat and pulled it onto his bare head. He searched through the wrecked filing cabinets and storage drawers and painstakingly chose each item before loading everything into a plastic bag and into the back of the van. As he drove away deep in thought, he subconsciously pushed his tongue around the inside of his mouth and sucked at his lips. *He was on a mission.*

It was dark when he arrived at the bank. He parked at the rear of the converted Victorian building and rummaged around in the back of the van. He removed a tin of spray paint pulled on a pair of Craig's company overalls pulled the beanie hat down over his forehead and calmly walked to the front of the bank and as though he had all the time in the world. He carefully sprayed the wall with offensive slogans and drawings taking care to deliberately misspell some of the words.

He stood back and admired his work and smiled to himself. Satisfied with his handiwork he climbed back into the van and drove back into town.

Brian drove slowly into the new estate of detached houses checking each car as he passed. He recognised Pam's VW parked in the drive and stopped directly outside of her house and waited. Within a few minutes he saw the bedroom curtains twitch. He climbed out of the van and stood in the shadows near the front door with his back to the door.

The door opened and Pam whispered to him excitedly. 'Craig . . . what a lovely surprise . . .'

Brian moved into the light, turned and stood facing her.

'Bri . . . ?'

She took a step back and made to close the door but he was too quick. He forced his way in and stood in the centre of the living room, his paint covered shoes sinking deep into the thick pile carpet. The lights were dimmed and several perfumed candles filled the whole house with the fragrance of vanilla. The expensive dark brown leather suite, designer coffee table, matching side tables and ornate glass table lamps gave a peaceful feel to the room. The walls were papered with a warm orange textured Laura Ashley paper, which matched the pattern on the curtains and cushions.

It was the first time Brian had seen Pam outside of the office and she looked very different indeed. Her blonde hair, which she had always worn in a French plait, now hung over her naked shoulders. She wore a sheer chemise embroidered with pink and blue silk butterflies and a matching robe. She pulled the robe around her and crossed her arms.

Brian remained in the centre of the room, removed his woollen hat and waited for what seemed like several minutes before he finally spoke.

'Hello, Pam . . . sorry to disappoint you—'

'What?'

Brian teased her and repeated himself very slowly. 'I said . . . I'm sorry to disappoint you'.

She looked fixedly at him and tried to comprehend the transformation, the bright red veins which ran across his eyes, the unshaven tired face and shaved head. She took a deep breath and shook her head anxiously as she spoke. 'Brian, what on earth has happened to you?' She looked him up and down and dragged out her few words. 'You've . . . changed,' she said softly.

Brian rubbed his eyes, raised his hands, turned them palm up and waited.

Pam reached for the bottle of red wine.

'Do you want a drink?'

Brian shook his head.

'No thanks'.

She looked at him and squinted. 'What did you do to your hair?'

Brian raised his shoulders and shook his head.

Her face suddenly drained of all colour. 'You've got Craig's van and . . . you're wearing his overalls . . .' she said anxiously.

He smiled at her before he spoke. 'Yeah,' he said cockily.

She looked across at her mobile phone and made to move towards it.

Brian picked it up and slid it into his pocket, shook his head and muttered under his breath. He frowned at her. 'You haven't heard?'

She trembled slightly and sat on the settee. 'Heard what?'

'My house has been repossessed . . . I'm broke!' He tilted his head. 'I've lost everything . . . and I mean *everything*,' he said pensively.

'How can you say that, Brian?'

He suddenly flipped.

'I've been shafted by everybody!' He kicked out at the settee and screamed at her. 'How long?'

She ignored his question.

'You know you still have friends . . . me and Jackie would do anything for you . . . you know that'.

He forced a smile.

'Do I?'

'We've been with you a long time . . .'

He smiled again.

'I know'.

She shot him a quizzical look.

'What?'

Brian remained motionless.

She played with her long hair with her left hand and with her other hand opened the top of the chemise to expose her pale breasts.

Brian screwed up his face in disgust.

'Fuck you!' he screamed.

She licked her lips.

'Do you want to?' she asked softly.

'Why do you think you can try this shit with me?' He spat down at her. 'It worked with Craig . . . the sad bastard . . .' He shook his head wildly. 'Me?'

She looked embarrassed but as she regained her composure she pushed herself to her feet and walked towards him. She screamed directly into his face. 'You bastard! Do you know Jackie would have done anything for you? I mean any-thing—'

'What?'

'Didn't you notice that?'

'Jackie?'

'Yeah . . .'

Brian was taken aback and his face reddened.

She smiled. 'Sitting as close to you as she could get without climbing all over you . . .' She laughed a crude laugh. 'She would have fucked you *anywhere . . . anytime*'.

Brian found it hard to contain his anger and he screamed at her. 'Enough of this shit!' He clenched his fists and continued. 'I asked *you* . . . how fucking long has this been going on?'

She smiled.

'. . . ah . . . you mean me and Craig?'

She moved across the room and picked up a framed photograph of her and Craig in an intimate Spanish bar and tapped the glass. 'Well . . . we had to keep it quiet . . .' She licked her lips. 'He is married . . . kids . . . You know . . . Never ends well does it?'

Brian looked at the photograph. 'How did the two of you get away with that? I mean going to Spain . . . together?'

'Easy . . .' She smirked at him. 'Craig and . . . what's her name?'

Brian thought and replied. 'Andrea . . .'

216

Pam continued. 'Well . . .' She shrugged. 'Whatever . . .' She took a huge gulp of wine. 'They both had a session of sun beds before *we* went away for the Bank holiday weekend so no one was any the wiser'. She sneered at Brian. 'I mean no one . . . no one,' she sneered. 'You didn't even suspect us'.

Brian said nothing but looked at her and waited.

'How long, Pam?'

She reached down and picked up her now empty wine glass from the table next to her armchair and poured herself another red wine. She held up the bottle.

Brian shook his head.

'Do you want something else . . . coffee?'

He shook his head again.

Pam gulped the wine and emptied the glass. She refilled it and emptied the bottle.

'So what were *your* plans?' he asked.

She swallowed hard and reached for the empty wine bottle but realising it was empty she placed it back on the table.

Brian continued. 'Run off to Spain? The two of you . . . ? Leave the sly bastard's wife!' He hesitated. 'Andrea . . . and the kids to fend for themselves?'

He brought his hand down hard on the table and the bottle fell to the floor spilling the last dregs of wine onto the beige carpet.

Her whole body stiffened and she pulled back.

'*Brian* . . . what has happened to you? Why have you shaved your head? Why?' She gathered her thoughts. 'How's Sylvia?'

She stood up and picked up the empty wine bottle.

He moved towards her and pushed his face against hers. 'Why do you give a fuck? Why the pretence?' He raised his voice. 'Why?'

She took a step back and fell heavily into the chair. She shook her head wildly and looked up at him.

Brian looked around the room at the opulent decadence.

'Well?'

Pam said nothing.

He pulled out the memory stick and held it up.

'Do you know what this is?'

She pushed herself deeper into the chair.

'I'll tell you what *this* is,' he said. He clicked at the cover with his thumb nail and pushed it towards her face.

She pulled away and turned her head.

'*This* tiny piece of plastic . . . cost less than a tenner . . . but it's worth a fortune to me,' he said.

She winced.

'Is it?' she murmured.

'I need to go to the toilet'.

She made to stand.

He pulled her back. 'When we've finished this . . . you can piss all you want!' he said as he glared at her. He reached across to the table and grabbed at her laptop.

'Do you want to see what I mean?' he asked.

Brian threw the laptop at her.

She caught it awkwardly and held it close to her chest.

'Fire it up . . . ! Go on!' he demanded.

She opened the cover and flicked the button. The screen lit up, she typed in her password and looked up at Brian.

He handed her the memory stick.

She trembled as she pushed it in and while she waited she drummed her perfectly manicured and brightly painted nails nervously on the keyboard.

'You didn't think I'd find out did you?' he asked.

'F . . . f . . . find out what?' she stuttered.

'Don't you know?'

'Know . . . ?' she murmured.

'Come on, Pam . . . you can't hide it any longer. Stop playing games'. He inched towards her, bent down and screamed directly into her ashen face. 'You fucking robbed me blind! That's what!'

'Me?'

She tried to stand but he pushed her back into the arm chair.

'Don't even try to explain. This is what you're going to do!'

He pulled a notebook from his pocket and leaned over the back of the armchair watching her every move. 'Log into the bank account,' he demanded.

She feigned ignorance.

Brian reached forward and screamed at her. 'Just fucking log in will yer or I swear I'll break your fucking arms!'

She shook violently as she turned her head and looked up at him.

'Log into the bank account . . . You know . . . **THE** bank account!'

She continued to stare back at him but didn't move.

'Just do it . . . or I swear . . . you're . . .' He stomped around the room picked up an ornate glass vase and threw it through the plasma screen. The screen exploded and shards of glass flew across the room and onto the carpet and furniture.

She shrieked with terror.

'Do it!' he screamed.

She feverishly typed on the keyboard and when the bank account appeared on the screen she stopped and looked up at him.

He looked at the screen and feigned a smile. What he saw made him kick out wildly at the furniture. He stopped suddenly and spun around to face her. 'Good . . . very good . . .' he said mockingly. He continued to breathe heavily, wiped the sweat from his face and dried his hands on his overalls. 'I think we understand each other now . . .' He paused and glared at her. 'Don't we?' he said with a slow knowing nod.

She bowed her head fervently.

He thrust the notebook directly in front of her.

'£75,000 into that account!'

He tapped his index finger impatiently against the account number and sort code on the page.

She hesitated and he raised his hand to her.

She input the details and paused yet again.

'Do it! Press transfer!' he screamed.

She made to transfer the money but fiddled with the keyboard as she attempted to play for time.

He screamed at her. 'Do it!'

She looked directly at him and clicked the keyboard without looking down.

He forced a satisfied smile as he saw the bank transfer go through. He seemed to relax briefly and he subconsciously stroked his shaven head before he gave her an enquiring look.

'Did Craig know?' he asked in a matter of fact way.

Pam didn't reply.

Her failure to reply angered him; he flicked the page and pointed at the second account information tapping the details impatiently.

'£40,000 . . . Do it!' he screamed.

His whole body shook.

Pam looked up at him nervously and trembled as she methodically clicked at the keys to transfer the money.

'Why the hell did you screw me and the company?' he asked.

'I knew you wouldn't miss it . . . you were so far up your own ass . . .' she replied coldly.

'What?' he raged.

'You had a family . . . kids . . . I had nothing'. She smiled and looked across at the photo. 'That was until Craig and me . . .'

He ignored her and turned another page and tapped it.

'£25,000!'

She clicked the cursor to transfer the money.

Brian waited for the transfer to be confirmed before he turned the fourth page and once again tapped on the page.

'£25,000!'

She obeyed him and waited for it to transfer.

'OK . . . Now how much is left? He asked anxiously.

She moved the cursor across the screen and clicked on it. She replied in little more than a murmur. 'Forty three thousand and fifty one pounds, twenty three pence,' she said as her voice tailed off to little more than a whisper.

He turned another page and pointed to the account information.

She looked up at him, desperation in her eyes.

'Do it! All of it! Do it now!' he screamed.

As she pressed the transfer button for the last time her home telephone rang. They both looked across at it.

'Answer it . . . I know it's the bank . . . 24-hour banking is wonderful isn't it?' He smirked at her. 'They want *you* to verify the transfers'.

She looked at him.

'They're more than ten grand . . .' he said knowingly.

The phone continued to ring and she looked at him defiantly.

Brian picked it up and thrust it into her hand. He moved close to her and listened to the caller.

Reluctant to answer the voice at the other end of the phone, Pam pulled away.

Brian grabbed her other arm and spoke through his gritted teeth. 'Do it!' he growled.

'Hello . . .' She nodded unconvincingly. 'Yes that's correct this is Pam Sterling'. She looked at Brian and considered how she could terminate the conversation.

Brian knew that and he twisted her arm up her back and squeezed it forcefully.

Pam gave them her password details and continued. 'Yes, the transfers are correct'. She squirmed and swallowed hard. 'No, we've decided to close the business'. She paused and took a deep breath. 'You know how it is . . . difficult times . . . the recession?'

Brian could hear the caller trying to convince Pam to think about her options and he fired her a threatening glare.

'N . . . no . . . no we've already made our decision'. Brian could see she wanted to scream out to the person at the other end but he squeezed her arm even harder. She winced with pain as she spoke. 'I've already told you . . .' She took a huge breath. 'We've made our decision. Thank you,' she said.

She let the phone drop, Brian reached out and caught it and placed it back on the table.

Brian grinned at her. 'Watching you then, made me wonder if you've ever been honest'.

Pam looked mindlessly back at him.

'How long *have* you been screwing me?' asked Brian.

'A month after I started,' she replied smugly.

Brian glared at her.

'You let *me* go through all that shit? He punched at the air. 'Your . . . your . . . your . . . fucking tears and concern . . .' He shook his head wildly and made to move towards her but stopped a few feet from her chair. 'Christ! All of that . . . was a total fucking sham!'

She looked directly at him and laughed.

'It was easy,' she mocked.

Brian twitched with rage. His whole body stiffened and the veins bulged across his temple. He was unable to speak and glared at her as she continued.

'I formed a new company . . . Brian Chapman Services (UK) Limited'. She waited for Brian's reaction.

His face whitened with total shock and disbelief.

Pam continued. 'After that it was a piece of cake. I used different sub-contractors to do the work and I invoiced it through that company and was paid by bank transfer. Sometimes I even banked your cheques . . .' She continued to antagonise him and snarled through her teeth as she spoke. 'I could have had hundreds of thousands if I'd wanted but I wasn't greedy—'

'Greedy! You're a robbing bastard! A fucking thief!'

He grabbed the laptop and threw it into the fireplace and stamped on it, smashing it beyond recognition. 'I'd still be in business if you hadn't robbed me blind!'

She pushed herself out of the chair, walked unsteadily to the kitchen and returned with a new bottle of wine. She unscrewed the top, poured another full glass and gulped it down. She stood and stared hard at him, her eyes cutting deep into him. 'Do you know what?' she slurred. 'You ruined the business yourself . . . Your grandiose ideas . . . fucking video . . . new vans . . . the list is endless!' She refilled the glass and stiffened before she continued. 'I said . . . you . . . ruined . . . yourself!' She poked him hard in the chest. 'Do you understand?' she said as she gasped for air.

Brian raised his hand and held it in mid-air. 'Tell me . . . what did you expect to do with it?' He paused. '*My* company's money?'

'Me and Craig have something special,' she said glibly.

Brian forced an inane smile. 'Is that right?'

She replied sharply. 'Yeah . . . we do'.

'Oh really?' His top lip curled. 'Where do you think that cheating bastard is tonight?'

Pam screwed up her face and stared back at him. 'He's at home!' She thought long and hard before she continued in a subdued voice. 'You know Brian . . . you're such a callous bastard!'

He turned his back on her and began to walk towards the kitchen.

'Me?' he growled. 'Just look at yourself'. He turned suddenly. 'He's not at home—'

'What?'

He smirked at her as he walked slowly back towards her.

'I told you he's *not at* home'.

'Wh . . . where is he?'

'Doing what he seems to do best . . . shagging!'

'I don't believe you!'

'You know he's a total shit . . . I should have got rid of him months ago—'

'Why didn't you?' she retorted angrily. 'You had your chances . . .'

'Um . . .'

Brian paced around the room before he unexpectedly moved towards her.

'So answer *my* question . . . Where the hell do you think the shagging bastard is tonight?'

'After what you did to him today he'll be at home,' she said defiantly

She pushed herself out of the chair and tried to stand but began to rock precariously from side to side.

'Why *did* you treat him like that?' She stopped suddenly and screwed up her face. '. . . and what the hell are *you* doing with *his* van?' she slurred.

'I reckon I paid for it? Don't you?'

She tripped and fell spilling red wine onto the already stained carpet.

Brian picked her up and threw her into the arm chair. He scribbled a message in his note book, took her mobile from his overall pocket, fiddled with it and then thrust it in front of her.

'Do it!'

She pulled away from him.

He grabbed her arm.

'I said . . . Do it!'

She gingerly tapped in the message and Brian put her mobile into his top pocket.

'You bastard,' she growled.

Brian glared back at her.

'I think you've got off lightly . . . don't you?'

Pam didn't reply.

'Whichever way you look at it . . .' He gave her a wry smile. 'It's still fraud . . . I mean you could get at least five years for that'. He paused. 'And who do you think *he'll* be shagging while you're in there?'

Pam refilled her glass and immediately emptied it. She looked up at him and tried to focus through her drunken eyes as she mumbled her unintelligible response.

Brian took one last look around the room and as he turned he noticed something on the side table. He reached out and grabbed the pearl inlaid letter opener that Sylvia had given him when they started the business. He rushed towards her held it menacingly against her throat.

For the first time Pam cowered in absolute terror.

'You thought you could buy part of my life for a *fiver*?' he screamed.

She twisted her head and looked at him open mouthed as her bottom lip began to tremble uncontrollably. 'Three pounds,' she murmured drunkenly.

Brian slipped the letter opener into his shirt pocket and feigned a laugh as he continued. 'You're welcome to the rest of the crap you bought in that box'.

His expression suddenly changed to a look of sheer contempt, he grabbed at her and threw her back into the arm chair and then tipped it backwards. Pam fell against the wall and the armchair pinned her against the wall. Brian ripped the phone from the wall and smashed it to pieces before he tore out the connection box.

She tried to stand and slumped back onto the upturned armchair.

'How did you know?' she asked slurring every word.

His face broke into a theatrically posed smile.

'Um . . .' His face changed and he glared at her. 'Well there was a two hundred and seventy three pound payment unreconciled'. He scratched at his bare head. 'I didn't recognise our invoice number'. His nails dug deeper into his shaven head and it began to ooze blood. 'It just didn't seem right,' he said as he looked at the blood on his hand and rubbed it between his fingers.

Pam waited for him to continue but when he failed to speak she tried to reach the wine bottle.

'Well?' she slurred.

Brian looked down at her.

'Well what?'

'Did you know?'

He gave her a look of utter contempt.

'Nah . . . I had no idea . . .' He shook his head. 'It was just a hunch-''

'What?' she screamed.

She pushed herself up and as she tried to hit out at him she tripped on the coffee table and fell heavily onto the carpet.

Brian raised his bloodied hand, looked down at her and snarled.

She pulled back in fear.

He continued to mutter obscenities as he walked out of the front door slamming it violently behind him.

Brian drove back to his car removed his laptop from the van and locked it in the boot. He then drove the van back to Natasha's flat and parked it in full view of the third floor bedroom window. He grabbed at the beanie hat pulled it off his bloodied head and ripped it into pieces. He removed three cans of paint thinners from the van and soaked some of the rags in it before he poured the remainder over the tyres and bonnet.

He took a tube of superglue from his pocket and squeezed it into each door lock. He removed the filler cap and pushed some of the rags he'd picked up at the store into the fuel tank before he took off the overalls and gloves and pushed them on top of the tyres jamming them under the wheel arches. He placed a rolled up newspaper in a paint pot directly beneath the end of the trailing rags and lit it.

He crept back to his car, started the engine and watched as the flames in the pot licked around the base of the rags. He waited for a split second and then drove quietly away and stopped at the end of the street. Maintaining a clear view of the van and flat he waited. When he saw the fire lapping around the fuel tank he dialled Natasha's number. Once he'd sent the text he ripped the battery and Sim card from Pam's mobile and threw it out of the car.

Brian knew this would cause Craig a massive problem with Natasha.

It did.

Natasha picked up Craig's mobile as soon as it bleeped and she read the message.

'Hello, Craig darling will you be over tonight?
The bed's warm . . . and I'm waiting.
Pam XXXX'

Within a few minutes Craig opened the front door and hobbled painfully towards his van. The top floor window opened and Natasha screamed down at him. He ignored her. His priority was to get to the van. But before he could reach the van the overalls and gloves caught fire igniting the tyres and engulfing the van in flames. The fire continued to rage and a massive explosion blasted pieces of metal and glass high up into the air. Craig was knocked to the ground and he lay on the pavement unconscious.

Brian thought to himself. *What had he done? What had he become?*

As he drove away he forced a bitter and satisfied smile.

The fire completely destroyed the van and its contents and with it Craig and Pam's impossible dream.

CHAPTER TWENTY-FIVE

We gotta get out of this place

Sylvia sat in silence and watched the musicians going through the same songs they had played every week. In fact, they played the same songs every week in the same order and she knew when they began to sing, *She'll be coming 'round the mountain,* it was the time to make her move. While everyone joined in on the final rousing chorus she got up unnoticed and walked down the corridor to the coat rack. She carefully selected the brightest jacket she could find.

The yellow and black check oversized jacket was perfect.

She picked her way through the hats on the pegs and chose a dark purple knitted hat. She pulled it onto her head, grabbed her long white hair and pushed it up in under and slipped into the coat. She returned to the music room and waited. She felt for and shook the tube of tablets, her prescribed medication, and tightened her fist around the container.

When the musicians finished she grabbed a tambourine and maracas and mingled with them as they packed the remainder of their instruments. The patients often spent time with them following the afternoon session but today the musicians appeared to want to leave much quicker than normal. As they moved towards the door the large woman lunged out at another patient. They were joined by three more patients who immediately struck out wantonly at each other. Their high pitched screams built to a crescendo as they bit and kicked each other and rolled across the floor.

The nearest nurse screamed out. 'Fire! Fire!'

It was a code that they only used a few times each year but something that indicated there was a real emergency.

The nurse was joined almost immediately by more nurses, carers and supervisors who tried desperately to split the patients up. The entertainers picked their way between the combatants and walked out of the room and down the corridor. Sylvia mixed with them and while the group leader collected their fee from the office the others walked through the revolving door and out to the minibus. Sylvia looked directly ahead and while they discussed the fracas she continued to walk with them unnoticed.

They carefully packed the instruments in the back of the van. Sylvia handed them the tambourine and maracas and drifted towards the edge of the car park and into the tree line.

While they waited for their leader, the musicians leaned against the mini bus, openly rolled spliffs and lit them.

A taxi arrived and dropped off a young woman in the car park. While the driver called in for his next job Sylvia approached him.

He wound down the window.

'Are you going into town?' she asked softly.

He smiled a broad smile. 'Well . . . yeas . . . jump in'. He reflected. 'Saves me going back empty . . . gotta watch the fuel costs these days . . .'

Sylvia nodded to him.

'Have to watch every penny now,' he said.

Sylvia looked at him unable to speak as a gust of wind took her breath away.

'Well come on, dear . . .' He drummed his fingers impatiently on the steering wheel. 'Do you want to go or not?'

She reached into the jacket pocket and froze. She stuttered anxiously. 'I . . . I . . . I'.

She opened her hand to reveal a packet of unopened chewing gum and mumbled at him incoherently. 'No money . . .'

The driver wound up the window and drove off, his tyres throwing up the gravel against her bare legs.

She didn't feel any pain.

She stood and watched as the taxi disappeared into the thick heavy mist rolling in off the sea and engulfing the trees and car park. She shivered as the wind blew and as the temperature suddenly plunged she crouched uncomfortably between the rows of parked cars and waited.

A white Nissan Micra drove into the car park and came to a halt. A young woman got out, leaned into the car and glared at the two teenage girls in the back seat. 'He *will* want to see you!' she screamed. 'You should come and see your grandfather!' She slammed the door. 'I won't be long . . . Just listen to the radio . . . and no fighting!'

She turned back and pushed her face hard against the side window. 'Understand!'

They both nodded submissively.

Sylvia peered between the parked cars and watched.

When the woman reached the top step the two girls sprang out of the car, slammed the doors and raced to join her.

*

As the musical group's vehicle pulled away the deep throbbing sound of Jamaican roots reggae boomed out of the open windows the passengers smiled to each other as their special cigarettes took effect and they suddenly became animated.

Sylvia seized the moment.

She crept warily towards the Micra and when she reached the car she looked furtively around before she opened the driver's door and slid into the seat. To her surprise the key was still in the ignition and the radio played. She took several short deep breaths before she turned the key. The car started first time and she pushed in the clutch, selected first gear, pressed the accelerator and the car jerked forward. She took her foot off the accelerator and took more deep breaths before edging steadily forward and out of the car park.

As she drove between the open metal gates she suddenly felt terrified. She wanted to look back but couldn't. She had absolutely no idea where she was and was left with no option but to follow the cliff top road as she struggled to make out the road through the ever thickening sea mist. While she continued to keep her eyes on what she could see of the road. She reached down blindly and fumbled with the buttons until she was able to turn off the radio.

There was silence; the first for many weeks.

Sylvia drove to Jenny's school pulled up a few yards from the entrance and switched off the engine.

Jenny was one of the last children to leave the school and she ran out with Lucy, her best friend. Lucy's mother was standing outside the gate and they rushed towards her.

Sylvia thought to herself. *Jenny looked so happy. Not a care in the world.*

She started the car and edged her way towards them and pulled up against the kerb.

Lucy's mother moved protectively between the car and the young girls.

Sylvia wound down the window. 'Hello, Gina,' she said softly.

Lucy's mother looked warily at Sylvia.

Sylvia spoke again. 'Gina, it's me, Sylvia'.

Lucy's mother stared at her hard, her concern very apparent.

Jenny and Lucy ran off along the pavement.

'Girls, just wait for me will you!' she screamed.

The young girls stopped and walked slowly back towards the car.

'I've come to pick up Jenny . . .' said Sylvia her voice faltering with nerves.

Lucy's mother moved towards the car and scanned Sylvia's face.

Sylvia removed her hat and her white hair cascaded across her face. She pulled it back from her eyes and forced a nervous smile. 'Gina . . . it is me . . .' she said the desperation in her voice causing her to stutter. 'Sylvie . . .'

Gina looked at Jenny then back to Sylvia before she spoke. 'How are you?' she asked.

'I've been ill . . . very ill . . . but I'm better now . . .' She paused. 'You know how it is?'

Gina forced a smile and gave a half-hearted response. 'Right . . . I see . . .' She sighed as she exhaled. 'OK'. She looked across at Jenny. 'Well . . . if you are all right . . .' she paused. 'How's, Brian?'

Sylvia smiled a lying smile before speaking. 'Brian . . . oh Brian's fine . . . He's fine'.

She looked at Gina and waited.

Gina looked back at her deep in thought.

'Jenny?' said Sylvia.

Gina took Jenny's hand and edged her towards the car. 'Jenny, your mummy's here for you'.

Jenny looked at the car and then at Sylvia and for an instant didn't recognise her but when Sylvia smiled Jenny jumped towards the window and gave her a huge kiss.

'Come on then . . . Get in . . . We're going home,' said Sylvia excitedly finding it impossible to hide her excitement.

Jenny climbed into the back seat and fastened her seat belt. 'Why are you wearing those strange clothes, mummy?' she asked.

Sylvia laughed the question away.

Before she pulled away Sylvia studied her face in the rear view mirror and for the first time saw her reflection. She shrank back with shock as she followed the deep lines in her face with the forefinger. Her face was drawn, pale and haggard. Her once dark shiny hair was white and straight and fell limp and dry onto the ridiculous jacket.

She closed her eyes, took a deep breath and pulled away.

Jenny was so excited she fired a succession of innocent questions at her mother. 'Are we going home, mummy? Will daddy be home . . . and Sammy? She fidgeted excitedly in her seat and then smiled the broadest of smiles. 'I haven't seen Sammy for ages. Are we really going home or will we all be staying at Nan's?'

Sylvia didn't answer she was too preoccupied in trying to find her way home.

*

Sylvia drove down the road and as she turned the corner she saw the TO AUCTION sign in her garden. She braked hard and stalled the car, narrowly missing a pedestrian who was stepping off the pavement. 'Wha . . . ?' she screamed.

'Careful, mummy . . . you could have killed her!' shrieked Jenny.

Sylvia flicked the ignition key drove into the drive and let the car shudder to a standstill. She sat looking at the sign and then the house. Metal sheets covered the front door and every window, the garden was overgrown and paper and cardboard littered the once pristine lawn and perfect rose bed.

Her house looked derelict.

'What the hell is going on?' she asked herself, as she punched wildly at the steering wheel. 'I don't believe it,' she said her voice cracking with a combination of fear, anger and emotion.

Jenny began to cry.

'Stay there, Jenny . . . I won't be a minute!' she said harshly.

Jenny tried to undo the seat belt.

'I told you wait there . . . in the car!' she screamed.

Jenny sobbed uncontrollably.

Sylvia got out of the car and checked that she was at the correct house by looking around at the neighbouring houses and her garden. She tilted the large ceramic plant pot near the front door and felt for the spare key.

She smiled when she found it. She reached up to the metal sheet covering the front door and made a futile attempt to push in the key.

The key didn't fit.

She rubbed it between her fingers and tried again. She cussed as she tried again; and again.

She tried to force it.

She failed.

She threw the key into the garden and stomped back to the car.

Jenny was out of control. She was inconsolable.

Sylvia ignored her and sat staring at the sign, transfixed.

Suddenly she shook her head wildly. She couldn't control herself and sobbed hysterically until she finally heard Jenny's screams. 'Sorry, Jenny . . . I'm really sorry darling . . . mummy's upset too . . . I'm so sorry . . .'

Jenny released herself from the rear car seat belt and slid into the front passenger seat.

They both cuddled and continued to sob in each other's arms.

Jenny subconsciously probed beneath the dashboard and pulled out a mobile phone.

Sylvia snatched it from her.

She dialled and waited. 'Come on Brian . . .' she cursed. 'Will you answer your phone?' She redialled and waited. 'Brian . . . where are you?'

She started the car and gunned the accelerator wildly as she reversed out of the drive, hitting the sign, causing it to tilt precariously, before racing out onto the road into the path of an oncoming delivery van.

The driver raised his fist to her and pressed his horn wildly as he screeched to a standstill within a few feet of her car.

'Mummy! What are *you* doing? You're going to have an accident if you're not careful,' shrieked Jenny.

Sylvia shook her head and accelerated away without acknowledging her or paying any attention to the lorry driver and the other drivers in the cul de sac. She gathered her thoughts and drove across town. As she drove through street after street the car started to jerk erratically. She glanced down at the dashboard and the amber petrol warning light that flashed back at her.

She drove across town and finally pulled up outside the terraced house, pulled on the handbrake and jumped out of the car. She hammered on the door and rang the bell simultaneously.

'Hold your horses will yer!' cursed the voice inside.

The woman opened the door and took a step back. Her face drained of all colour as she looked intently at Sylvia. Her voice faltered. 'Sylvia . . . is *it* you?'

Sylvia nodded.

Mrs Chapman gathered her thoughts before she continued. 'Sylvia, what's going on dearie? I thought you were in hospital'.

Sylvia blurted out her questions in quick succession without attempting to take a breath. 'I couldn't stand it any longer. Have you seen Brian? I can't get in the house . . . there's a for auction sign in the garden'.

'There's a what?' asked Mrs Chapman.

'I can't stop now. I . . . I . . . I've got to find Brian,' she gasped.

Mrs Chapman looked at her and tried to take in what was happening.

'I can't explain now . . .' said Sylvia as she gasped for air. 'Do you have any money? She looked around nervously expecting the doctors and nurses to come for her. She continued. 'I need to buy petrol'. She twitched nervously. 'I need to find, Brian . . .' Her hands trembled and her head twitched nervously.

'Course, dearie . . .' said, Mrs Chapman. She reached out to Sylvia. 'Come in—'

'I can't . . .' replied Sylvia shaking her head wildly as she forced a smile.

'Hang on a minute,' said Mrs Chapman

Mrs Chapman returned with her purse. She took out all the notes and the pound coins and held them out in front of her.

'Will that do?' she asked.

Sylvia snatched the notes and thrust them into her pocket before she rushed back to the car and started the engine. She wound down the window. 'Can Jenny stay with you?' she asked.

'Yes, of course,' said Mrs Chapman. She turned to her granddaughter. 'Come on, Jenny shall we make some cakes?' She reached out and took Jenny's trembling hand.

'You said we were going home, mummy . . .' Jenny stamped her feet. 'You lied!'

Brian's mother hugged Jenny tight.

'Come on, dearie . . . we'll make some cakes . . . and you can lick the spoon'.

Jenny looked up at her, wiped her eyes and forced a smile before waving to her mother. 'Be careful,' she mouthed.

'We'll be alright, Sylvia. Just let me know how you get on, won't you? I shall be worried to death until I hear from you,' she said.

Sylvia ignored her. 'If you hear from Brian, can you ask him to call me?' said Sylvia. She thought for a split second then continued. 'No, on second thoughts, ask him to wait here until I get back'.

As the car jerked and jolted down the road Mrs Chapman shouted after her. 'What shall I tell, Brian?

CHAPTER TWENTY-SIX

Without you

Brian revisited the office building and parked his car. He looked up at the two men who were fixing the 'SOLD' sign across the split company name board. As he read it he felt sick to his stomach. He regained his composure and walked slowly towards the building. He looked into the back window at the works office and then made his way to the front and peered into the general office. It had been stripped bare and the walls redecorated in magnolia. He stood and remembered the activity that had filled the office just a few weeks earlier. He pushed himself away from the window and walked around to the rear car park and made his way to the only car in the car park; his car. He watched as the workmen put the last few fixings into the side of the building. One of them nudged the other and shouted out naively. 'Hi, Brian . . . are you OK?'

Brian lifted his arm to acknowledge him, yanked at the car door until it finally opened. He took one last look at the building and pulled away.

He could hardly see as the tears rolled down his cheeks. He

found it hard to follow the road and see the oncoming traffic through his swollen eyes as he drove out of the city towards the country.

Sylvia drove into the company car park and drove up to the two men were loading their ladders onto the roof of their van. She wound down her window. 'Have either of you seen Brian Chapman?' she shouted.

'Who?' asked the older man.

The second man spoke. 'I saw him earlier,' he said proudly. 'I've known Mr Chapman for years. I've done the odd job for him ya know'.

Sylvia wasn't interested.

'What time was that?' she asked desperately.

'Oooooohh, mmmmm'. He looked at his watch. '. . . 'bout half an hour ago'. He scratched his head and gave her a confused look. 'Strange really, he was driving an old green Astra'.

Brian drove along the bypass and out into the country. Sammy sat excitedly in the passenger seat, looking out of the window, his saliva running down the glass as Brian drove into the woodland car park and chose an isolated space beneath the pine trees.

To protect the habitat for the local wildlife the Forestry Commission had permitted limited access to the area. The restricted number of car parking spaces in the forest had been carefully arranged amongst the trees in clusters of two and three to maintain the natural appearance. Instead of concrete parking bays they had been tastefully filled with granite dust. The grass and ferns had grown into the spaces removing the straight lines created by man.

The music faded. 'Here is the four o'clock news,' said the newsreader. 'Interest rates have been held at a half of one percent for yet another month.'

Brian sighed, reached out blindly and stroked Sammy.

'Prime Minister, David Cameron has assured everyone that he will do everything possible to get us through these difficult times—'

Brian reached out blindly and switched it off.

There was total silence.

Brian reflected on what had been and what might have been.

He suddenly flipped. 'The bastard . . . bloody bastard!' he screamed. 'What does he take us for? A load of fucking idiots! How much longer does he think he can keep repeating the same garbage over and over?'

Brian reached for the door handle and after lowering the door glass he finally opened the door.

Sammy jumped across him and raced around excitedly in the ferns and long grass. Brian followed him and made his way aimlessly through the woodland oblivious to everything around him. He walked for almost a mile before he turned and walked blindly back to the car. He looked around the deserted car park and up into the trees and wiped the tears from his eyes. He opened the boot and took out a length of rubber hose, pushed it onto the exhaust pipe and slipped it through the rear fanlight window. He returned to the car, closed the door and pulled up the window and while Sammy ran around the car and desperately tried to get in he switched on the engine.

Brian used Sylvia's phone and called his mother.

'Hi, mum, it's Brian'.

She could hear the wretchedness and desperation in his voice.

'Where on earth are you . . . ? We're all worried, Brian . . . Where are you?' she pleaded.

'I'm alright,' he lied.

He sobbed uncontrollably.

'Brian! Brian! Talk to me! Come on,' She screamed as she tried to control her emotions but knew for once she had to let go.

There was a lengthy silence.

'I've made such a mess of everything, mum . . . everything I've touched. I'm a useless . . .' He paused. 'A worthless piece of shit—'

'Brian, you've got a wonderful family and Sylvia dotes on you . . .' She tried desperately to reassure him and tried to pick her words. 'How can you say that?'

He ignored her. 'I've sorted out the money I borrowed—'

'What? Who cares about that? It's only money'.

He shouted at her. 'Well I do!'

'I told you the house would be yours anyway . . . so that's that'.

He took a deep breath and inhaled the deadly exhaust fumes.

Are you alright, Brian? Why don't you come over and have a cup of tea . . . and we can talk about it,' she pleaded.

'It's too late for that now, mum'. He wiped his eyes. 'I've messed up big time'.

'Brian . . . everything can be sorted out . . . You know that. I had to pick myself up after your dear dad died'.

He could hear the distress in her voice and he hated to do it.

243

But he continued. 'Anyway, the money's sorted . . . it should be in your bank by now—'

'What? How did you manage to do that?' She thought before she continued. 'You haven't robbed anyone have you?'

'Not exactly . . . someone robbed me . . .' He thought back to how long he had trusted Pam and how she had been screwing him and Sylvia for years. 'I've put some money into Jenny and Jamie's building society accounts and—'

'Brian . . . what have you done? What on earth are you talking about?'

He ignored her. 'And I've done the same for Sylvia . . . it's not a lot but it will help—'

'Brian, Brian . . . what on earth is going on? Where are you?' she pleaded desperately.

As the fumes continued to replace the air in his lungs he struggled to breathe. 'Sorry, mum . . . I've got to go . . . Love you . . .'

'Brian!'

'Please tell Sylvia, Jenny and Jamie I love them and . . .' His voice faltered. 'I lied to you . . . Sylvia wasn't in the hospital . . . she was sectioned!' He sobbed wildly. 'She's in Gresham . . . Gresham House!'

She screamed out. 'Brian . . . Brian . . . Brian, I've just see—'

The phone went dead.

Brian pushed in a cassette and cried hysterically.

Sylvia drove along the bypass and down the dual carriageway and turned into the country lane. She stopped periodically to resend her texts and call Brian without any success.

His mobile phone was dead.

She accelerated into the woodland car park racing across

the dried leaves, gravel and broken twigs. She jumped out of her car and ran through the woodland car park until she saw Sammy pawing wildly at the door and window of the green Astra in an isolated area on the far edge of the forest.

When Sammy saw Sylvia he raced towards her before returning to Brian's car. He rushed around it and pawed wildly at the doors. He briefly turned to look at Sylvia before he raced around the car and continued to paw and scratch erratically at the driver's door.

'Sammy!' she screamed, as she rushed towards the car.

She looked into the car and didn't recognise Brian.

She ran around the car, looked through the windscreen and twisted her head. Despite his shaven head Sylvia finally realised it was Brian slumped motionless in the driver's seat.

She tried the driver's door but it wouldn't budge.

'Brian!' she screamed.

There was no response.

She tugged at the hose pipe and dragged it out through the window. She rushed around to the other side and following a number of attempts to release it, the passenger door finally swung open.

'Brian . . . what the?'

He didn't move.

She screamed out. 'Brian!'

There was no movement.

She called out again, shook him as hard as she could and waited.

Brian slowly turned to face her. 'Sylve?' he murmured.

Tears ran down his cheeks and he sobbed hysterically. 'What have I done?' he mumbled.

'I didn't know what to think. I thought you'd . . .' She

stopped in mid-sentence as her tears flowed uncontrollably, blurring her sight.

Brian shook his head. 'Sylv, but . . .'

Sylvia threw her arms around his neck. 'Don't worry, love,' she trembled. 'We've got through things before . . .'

Sammy forced his way into the car and tried to get between them.

Sylvia continued. 'I'm sure we can do it again . . .' She stopped herself and looked lovingly into his swollen eyes and stroked his shaven head. 'That is if you want to?'

He looked at her unable to think or speak.

'You know we can do whatever we want,' she gushed.

She pulled out the mobile, pressed it and waited for a reply.

'He's alright . . . Yes . . . We're all fine,' she said to Brian's mother.

She clicked the mobile and threw it into the bracken and pulled at his hand.

Sammy raced backwards and forwards sensing that things were going to be alright.

'Do you know what it is today?' she asked.

He gave her a blank look.

'It's your birthday, Brian?'

He didn't acknowledge her.

Sylvia looked sad.

'I haven't got you a present . . . or even a card'.

'Who cares?' he said.

He looked back at the Micra and turned to her.

'Where did you get that car?'

She replied with a wide grin.

'I stole it . . .' She giggled. 'Aren't I naughty?'

'Come on . . . let's go for a walk. It's the one thing that doesn't cost us . . . No one can stop us doing that'.

She smiled at Brian and kissed his shaven head. '. . . and we'll get that house . . .' she said.

They held each other tight before they walked off into the woods.

Epilogue

On Wednesday 9th February 2011 George Osborne announced that the big five banks had agreed to lend more than £160 billion pounds to UK companies over the coming twelve months . . .

'Liars!' snarled Brian.

He was correct because on Tuesday 24th May 2011 it was announced that lending by the big five bank had fallen short of their promises by £25 million a day. And for any monies they did lend they were charging many companies in excess of 12.7% interest.

HERE COMES THE NIGHT

A short story by
Graham Sclater

Here Comes the Night

Bobby lay on his sun bed and tried desperately to enjoy the warm Mediterranean sun as it beat down onto his pale body. Two weeks earlier the specialist had given him the all clear. But as the sun bore down on him he couldn't help thinking of the crazy night just a few months earlier when for the first time in his short teenage life he had finally begun to enjoy himself. Everything was good, a new job with prospects and Gemma, a girlfriend who adored him.

His mistake was to give in and take her to a club that he knew would cause him trouble.

They arrived at Mango's after a few drinks at the local pub, the Vadis Club had been chosen for the celebration of Gemma's birthday the following week, but because Bobby knew that he would be away that night they decided to do something different. Mango's was certainly different.

Bobby stood at the bar amongst what he considered to be mostly misfits, people that he now tried hard to avoid since getting his new job and meeting Gemma. As always, one thing led to another and within an hour they were talking to another couple, George and Julie, who effectively forced two capsules onto them. Refusing to take any payment except a drink Bobby considerately bought another round of drinks as a way of thanking them and the couple swallowed the pills.

An hour later the four of them were dancing, in a way that they Gemma and Bobby found hard to identify with, continuing until three o'clock in the morning. They lost all track of time and finally as the DJ played the last record they all danced their way out of the club. Neither of them remembered the short walk home but they both agreed that it had been different and fun.

At the last moment, Bobby's night away on Gemma's birthday was cancelled and they were able to spend the night together. Gemma having enjoyed the last night out persuaded Bobby to hold the party at Mango's. He tried to persuade her to change her mind but it was pointless, after all it was Gemma's birthday.

Within a few minutes of being in the club George approached them and seemed genuinely pleased to see them. He handed Gemma two capsules, she took them passed one to Bobby and together as though it was a ritual they each swallowed one, but this time George stood looking at her until she opened her handbag and handed over ten pounds. At first Bobby shrugged his shoulders but pleased to be home for Gemma's birthday gave her a kiss and guided her towards the dance floor. The night was perfect they kissed, drank and again reluctantly left the dance floor when the DJ played his final record.

As they collected their coats George walked towards them and invited them to a party at his flat. They both agreed. George let the lovebirds; as he constantly referred to them, sit in the back seat of his gold BMW. After a short drive they found themselves pulling into the car park of a luxury dockside development in the centre of town. George smiled as he opened the rear car doors and let them out. The nudges between Gemma and Bobby said it all; they were more than a little surprised at where George lived. At first they thought that it was some sort of joke but when he took a small black remote control from the glove compartment and pointed it at the security gates and they opened they knew that it was for real.

George's flat, was in fact a luxury apartment on the top floor, with breathtaking views across the bay, and from the balcony it was possible to look across the Bristol Channel. He offered them drinks and before they were finished he opened a small decorative inlaid box and offered Gemma the opportunity of sampling the contents. At first, she was nervous so he teased her. 'It's your birthday go on.' She looked at Bobby but he nodded to her and reluctantly she took two small white tablets swallowing them with her whiskey. George them opened a second box and tempted Bobby to take out several brightly coloured capsules and again swallow them with his brandy.

Within a few seconds Bobby fell asleep on the leather Chesterfield and Gemma soon became oblivious to what was happening to her as the room started to spin. Before she knew it George carried into his bedroom where he showed her no mercy.

While he slept, Bobby subconsciously heard the screams and he gradually came around and after gathering his thoughts, unsteadily, he rolled off of the settee and staggered towards the bedroom. George heard him coming and as Bobby staggered into the bedroom and stood looking at Gemma splayed out on the bed; George hit him hard over the head rendering him unconscious.

Almost asleep on the sun bed Bobby could hear footsteps approaching. Gemma tapped him on the shoulder. 'Have you had enough yet?'

Bobby looked up and smiled at Gemma as she helped him to climb into his wheel chair. Even now after several months he often lost control of his feelings and tears filled his eyes. 'Gemma, where would I be without you?'

'Come off it, it was you who saved me. Where would I be without you?'

Gemma had been given the date rape drug and had suffered terribly, but when Bobby entered the bedroom he had almost certainly saved her from a fate worse than death. But having been disturbed, in anger, George had thrown Bobby from the balcony of the building allowing Gemma the chance to escape.

Bobby was immediately taken to intensive care and it was several days before he regained consciousness. His back, and legs had been broken and, unable to walk; he was confined to a wheelchair for the rest of his life. Bobby hated the anticipation of waiting for the night, and the darkness, because as it began to get dark he relived the last moments of his once normal life.

What had started out as a celebration of their young lives had ruined them forever.

www.ingramcontent.com/pod-product-compliance
Lightning Source LLC
Chambersburg PA
CBHW070051260626
47160CB00004B/1168